MOTIONAL BLUR

In memory of Clair George

MOTIONAL BLUR

A Novel

ROBERT ERINGER

Skyhorse Publishing

Skyhorse Publishing books may be purchased in bulk at special discounts for sales promotion, corporate gifts, fund-raising, or educational purposes. Special editions can also be created to specifications. For details, contact the Special Sales Department, Skyhorse Publishing, 307 West 36th Street, 11th Floor, New York, NY 10018 or info@skyhorsepublishing.com.

Skyhorse® and Skyhorse Publishing® are registered trademarks of Skyhorse Publishing, Inc.®, a Delaware corporation.

Visit our website at www.skyhorsepublishing.com.

10 9 8 7 6 5 4 3 2 1

Library of Congress Cataloging-in-Publication Data is available on file.

Cover design by Laura Klynstra
Cover photo: iStock

Print ISBN: 978-1-5107-1114-3
Ebook ISBN: 978-1-5107-1115-0

Printed in the United States of America

1.

When I think about it now, it's like an old grainy black and white movie with a scratchy sound playing in my head. Sometimes, the memory makes me sad, other times, happy.

My name is Luke Andersen, and I was just about to turn thirty-nine when I got the call.

I'd had maybe the most normal day of my life. Slept in, which for me means about noon, unless the waves are whistling for me, which they weren't. The dawn patrol dudes were still at it when finally I hit the beach after a mini-burger and fries at Tinker's. Should have driven to Rincon, evaded the kooks, but I wasn't sure if I still had alcohol in my bloodstream from the night before. As usual, I'd been drinking *Jaime juice*: shots of Herradura tequila and Bud Light chasers at the west side bar where I would host karaoke twice a week to supplement my part-time driving income.

In fact, this was a Tuesday, a karaoke night, so I had to stay reasonably straight. Things took a negative downturn when I arrived at the bar past seven to set up the sound equipment.

Eric, the bartender, pulls me aside, out of earshot of our boss, Anal Breath, who thinks we're all in the marines.

"A sheriff's deputy stopped by looking for you," says Eric.

"You're kidding me, right?"

"No, man. He asked if you were here, and when I said you weren't, he wanted to confirm you work here and what hours."

"What did you tell him?"

"I said you're *on call,* no fixed hours."

"Right on. Did he say what it was about?"

"I didn't ask."

I sort of already knew. I'd gotten three jury duty letters over the last couple months. The fourth—if they're serious—gets delivered by a sheriff's deputy, and then you've got some *s'plaining* to do before a judge, who fines you a fortune for refusing to accept a civic job way below minimum wage, and if you don't show up for *that,* you're in contempt and they issue a warrant.

That's life as I know it: judges and lawyers get paid the serious *ka-ching* while surfer dudes like me make a buck-eighty-eight an hour for listening to some insurance company's lame excuse for not wanting to pay up.

Last time, about ten years ago, I got out of jury duty by saying I believe in *jury power*, which I do, meaning that if a law is dumb—like marijuana possession—I judge the *law* guilty, and acquit the accused no matter the evidence.

This time, I was planning to show up, I swear, get dismissed again the same way, but the waves that day were killer.

Halfway through the evening, I get a text from The Drive Cycle asking me to call in for a job.

I don't really want a job right now, on top of which I've already had two shots of Jaime juice and I'm waiting for my lame-o boss to split for the office upstairs and bone one of the female flies, so I can tap myself a brewski.

Then I get another text, and another saying if I don't call in, I'm history, and so I think, okay, doesn't hurt to call, tell them I'm over the limit, and that nails the situado dead.

So I hand the mic to a gal who's been singing and flirting with me all evening, and go outside, which gives me the opportunity to toke a spliff with a west side gangbanger—and why not, my birthday cuts in at midnight, the last in my thirties, and who the hell knows where my thirties went—or if I'd make it to forty.

"S'up?"

"Where've ya been, Luke?"

"My Tuesday gig at the bar, you know. Sorry, dude, couldn't hear the phone with Too-Tall singing the Bee Gees. Ugh."

"You're supposed to call in. We have a job for you."

"I've been drinking."

"No problem, the job is tomorrow morning."

"Aww, man, you know, it's my *birthday* tomorrow. Can't you get someone else?"

"He requested you."

"*Who* requested me?"

"The fare."

"Why me?"

A sheriff's deputy trap? No way, those dudes are numbskulls.

"Didn't ask. Maybe you drove him before, a referral—how the hell should I know? You got fans."

I doubt that very much.

"Airport run?" I'd get it done, get back in time for a wave or three, and grab a snooze late afternoon.

"Nah, this one's further. Vegas."

"*Vegas?* Aww, man . . . Why doesn't he fly? That's eleven hours there and back!"

"Like I said, he specifically requested you, which is perfect because I don't have anyone else."

"I can't do it."

"If you don't take it, I need the vehicle back, and we're done. Think about it and call me in fifteen."

"Son of a bitch!" I would have thrown my stupid smartphone against the wall but all I would've ended up with is a broken phone, and I couldn't afford the lousy fifty bucks I'd make this evening to fix it.

I go back in the bar. The gal I'd given the mic to is hogging it, making a butthole of herself, and I can see Anal Breath down the bar bristling like a warthog.

'Where've *you* been?" he snorts.

"On a break."

"You don't get a break. And you're not allowed to appoint a drunk to take your place."

"Who else, then? They're *all* drunk in this place."

"We'll talk about this tomorrow."

Oh, joy.

"I can be a real dick," he adds.

"We know."

"What's that supposed to mean?"

"Whatever."

I get karaoke back on track—a ballad, "Henry the Crooner," his no-cost therapy—lower the volume, and call my mother in Solvang. "S'up?"

"Luke, are you okay?" She wasn't used to hearing from me in the evening.

"Fine, Mom. I may have to drive to Vegas tomorrow on a Drive Cycle job, you know, but I don't want to."

"Why not?"

"It'll take all day—and it's my birthday, remember?"

"What does your supervisor say, Luke?"

"He says if I don't take it I've got to return their wheels."

She doesn't say anything in that single parent way of hers that makes me feel like I'm still eight years old, and maybe I am, but I like it that way. "Luke," she finally says, "you can't go on losing jobs. And you won't have a car anymore. You can celebrate the day after."

"Yeah, Mom, you're right."

I click off, still planning not to do it.

Through half-open saloon swing doors I glimpse a police cruiser pulling alongside the curb.

"Oh shit," I mutter. "He's back." I approach Anal Breath. "Gotta go."

"You kidding me? You've got another hour."

"Sorry."

"Sorry? Don't plan on getting paid tonight. Or coming back again. Ever."

I pull an exit-stage-left through the back door as Mr. Sheriff's Deputy enters through the front.

Fortunately, I'd left Abe—the Cycle's eight-year-old Lincoln Town Car—on a side road.

Unfortunately, Cheryl, the karaoke drunk, meets me there. "Hiding out from the bacon?"

"Early day tomorrow, you know."

"Expecting bombers?"

She's talking about big waves.

"Yeah."

She opens the door to her Honda.

"You shouldn't be driving," I say. "You drank too much."

"So did you!"

"No, just two shots, I'm good. You had about six. I'll drive you home."

She thinks about it a few seconds. "No, I can make it."

"Don't do it. Please? I'll drive you. Your car is safe here overnight."

"Maybe I'll go back in, sing a few more songs."

I knew she'd have a few more drinks instead—and then drive. "C'mon. I'll drive you. Where do you live?"

By the time we get across town and up onto the Riviera, her left hand is dangling between my legs.

When we stop, she nuzzles her lips into my ear, whispering, "You coming in?"

"I'd really like to," I say. "You're very attractive. But I gotta get up early tomorrow."

Truth is, I don't like taking advantage of women who've been drinking too much.

She bails, and I tap a key, connect to the Cycle.

"Luke?"

"Yo, dude. I'm sorry but . . ." Suddenly, a shooting star flares across the sky over the ocean. ". . . Whoa!"

"You all right?"

"Yeah. Wow, that was amazing!"

"What?"

"Never mind." And then I impulsively tell him I'll take the job even though I'd intended not to.

He gives me the pickup details, and I'm still wondering how my mind got changed, aside from that pesky sheriff's deputy.

"Eight thirty. And a specific request *not* to be late. Fuck it up like the last time and it's your last run."

Last time I'd overslept.

They know my own car needs a new transmission, so they think they have me by the balls, and they do.

2.

Next morning. No waves. No shots of Jaime juice. Just a grande Americano from Starbucks in a paper cup, waiting for my fare on the bricked forecourt of the Biltmore Hotel in Montecito.

At 8:33 precisely the right rear passenger door opens. I hadn't even seen anyone approach.

"Charles Gearhart," he says. "Would you care to open the trunk?"

I flick a switch and pop the sucker. I'm about to get out and help, but he's on it, so I sip my coffee, watch him remove his navy blazer, and settle into the backseat with an armful of newspapers.

"We're driving to Vegas, right, Mister Gearhart?" I connect my eyes with his in the rearview mirror.

"Yes."

"Any particular routing?"

There are only two choices, and both connect in Barstow for the rest of the way. We still have an eyeball gaze going.

He shrugs. "You choose."

I ease Abe onto Channel Drive and join the freeway, 101 South. Gearhart immerses himself in the *New York Times* and the *Wall Street Journal* and doesn't resurface until about an hour later when I'm about to get off I-5 and onto Route 14 toward Victorville, making good time.

"I gotta take a pit stop in Acton," I say. "It's the coffee."

"How much do you drink?" he asks.

"I like coffee."

"That's not what I asked."

Cute. I liked it better when he was stuck in newsprint.

"A few cups a day."

"You sleep okay with that?"

He was starting to sound like my mother, who still hadn't called to wish me happy birthday.

"It's having to wake up early that interferes with my sleep." That would hopefully shut him up.

Acton is a carnival of gas stations. I pull into Chevron—nice clean gas—feed Abe, a serious guzzler, take a whiz, and grab a bag of Rold Gold pretzels for the road.

"Need anything, Mister Gearhart?" I ask, adjusting my new wraparound Oakleys, an early present from my mom.

He shakes his head, studying me through the rearview mirror.

I study him back through mirrored glasses. He seems oddly familiar. I've seen him before, just can't figure where or when. Maybe on TV? Happens a lot in Santa Barbara, wannabes and has-beens—and sometimes the real thing in between.

The road is now lined on both sides by cacti and telephone poles, a hot sun blaring down on us. Thank the Lord for AC.

"You live in Vegas?" I ask.

"No."

"Like to gamble?"

"No."

"Going to see a show?"

"No."

I should have known there and then something else was going down. But I was just trying to make conversation, pass the time, so I gave it no further thought and retreated into my mind. Yeah, if nothing more, I'd fixed that sheriff's deputy with my absence today. He'd go to my home. *No one there.* Maybe back to the bar. *No longer works here.* After that, they'd give up. As if they didn't have something better to do.

Meantime, Gearhart dips into a large leather and canvas satchel beside him and grabs a book to read, something called *The Path* by Richard Matheson. He's wearing a button-down blue shirt and khaki trousers and the kind of burgundy loafers that have tassels. An East Coast look, his thick head of hair somewhere between red and gray; looks like he once had a shitload of freckles, the kind I hated when I was a kid.

At Barstow I need coffee.

Gearhart gets out to stretch and walk around, but that's it. (Strong bladder for an older dude.)

Then we're off again.

A couple hours later, Mr. Personality finally perks up. "What's that coming up ahead?"

"Nevada. It welcomes you with a casino at every border crossing, you know."

He stares at the cheapo gambling complexes in awe, one on each side of the road to catch comers *and* goers.

"You've never seen that before?" I ask.

Silence. I assume he isn't going to answer, but then: "I've seen a lot of the world. But not much of my own country. This looks tacky."

"Yup. You just defined Nevada. This will be your first time in Vegas?"

He doesn't answer, but continues his silence staring out the window while crossing the border, reminding me why I'd left my stash at home—Nevada is friggin' fascist when it comes to pot possession—another reason why I wanted to dump this old-timer and haul ass back to Summerland.

Gearhart catches my eye in the rearview mirror. "You're not carrying any marijuana are you?"

It's as if he's reading my mind and I freeze and my eyes feel like a deer about to be shot. How does he know about my habit? This is it, I'm going to get seriously busted, and I bet my own employer, the car service manager, is in on it, a full-on setup, maybe Anal Breath, too.

"No, I'm not," I squawk. I really wasn't, but I couldn't be sure about whatever crumbs are clinging to Abe in dark corners and crevices. "Why?"

"California may be okay with weed, but Nevada is the exact opposite."

So that's the plan—get me across into Nevada, carrying, lock me away forever!

3.

Finally, precisely five hours and twenty-three minutes since launching, the Vegas skyline looms. I can be back in time for buffalo wings and a potion at The Nugget.

Gearhart remains absorbed with his book.

"Shall I get off at the Strip?"

He looks up. "No. Keep going."

"You sure? Frank Sinatra Drive is the big one. What hotel you need?"

He doesn't say anything, just keeps reading his damn book. Maybe he's going to the convention center, North Vegas; he's certainly dressed for business.

Driving alongside the Strip, past the pyramid, New York New York, the High Roller Wheel, Harrah's, I joke, "We're running out of Vegas."

He doesn't answer, no expression, nothing.

"Can you at least tell me what road to take?" I finally say. "Because otherwise we're going to end up in Utah."

He finally puts his book down. "Good idea," he says.

"What?"

"I don't think I'd like Vegas. Utah sounds better."

I can't believe my ears. "You must be kidding me!"

"No. Let's go to Utah."

"*Where* in Utah?" Not that I have any intention of going there, but at this point I need to determine if I'm dealing with a mental case.

"Utah was *your* idea—you tell me."

"Utah wasn't *my* idea. I just said that's where we'd end up if we didn't get off in Vegas!"

"Okay, so let's end up there."

"Where?"

"Utah."

"Where in Utah?"

"Someplace where the sky doesn't fall."

I realize this conversation is going nowhere fast and that I'll need another opinion on this matter.

"Pit stop," I announce, nailing the last exit in North Vegas. "We need gas."

Maybe he'd finally get out to relieve himself and I'd leave him right here. But he says he doesn't have to go, and he doesn't budge from the backseat.

I pump gas, go inside for a whiz, and connect with headquarters.

"I'm in Vegas and Mister Gearhart has changed his mind, says he wants to keep driving, to Utah, but doesn't know *where* in Utah. What should I do, boss?"

"We have his credit card details on file, the cost to Vegas has already been authorized. Put him on and I'll get him to authorize another payment."

"But I don't want to go to Utah! I want to go home! The deal was Vegas!"

"Haven't you heard, the customer is always right?"

"Always *right*? He doesn't even know where he's going!"

"Let me talk to him."

I stare at my phone in disbelief. "Hold on." I return to Abe and climb behind the wheel, pass my phone to Gearhart. "My boss needs a word."

Gearhart takes the phone, listens, talks, listens, talks, hands my phone back. "He wants to talk to you."

I put the phone to my ear. "S'up?"

"You're going go Park City, Utah."

"*What?*"

"It just got prepaid."

I get out with the phone to my ear, walk toward the service station shop. "What the fuck? I gotta drive to Park City, Utah, now? That's another seven hours, for fuck's sake!"

"Best fare you've ever had."

"You're going to owe me big time. No, *overtime.*"

"He's taken care of that."

"What do you mean?"

"A big tip."

"Yeah, well right now I'm not feeling it. I feel like I'm getting boned. Where am I supposed to sleep tonight, in the car?"

"No, he's paying for a room at a hotel."

"*I'm* not sleeping in *his* room!"

"No. Your own."

"Whatever." I disconnect.

I'm tired and hungry and now I've got to drive to Utah, and then I've got to drive all the way back. Son of a bitch. On top that, I'm sick of trying to make conversation with this Gearhart guy, and now I'm pissed off at him, too, for screwing up my birthday, and my evening.

The road briefly meanders into Arizona before Utah appears with an eighty-mile-an-hour speed limit, which means ninety-five to me, though on clear stretches I push Abe to over one hundred, the passing landscape a motional blur.

Finally, Gearhart speaks up. "You're going to get a ticket."

"I know what I'm doing."

"Then why are you driving so fast?"

"I have a life I need to get back to."

"Tell me about that."

"About what?"

"Your life. And why you're so reckless with it."

"No danger here. It's all about *bursts* and *passing*. I hit it in bursts, when the road conditions are right and cops are nowhere to be seen. You pull enough bursts and it has a cumulative effect. But I always slow down when I overtake another vehicle. It shows respect to the other driver and demonstrates to any cops that you're driving safe."

"Gets you where you're going four minutes earlier?"

"More than that."

"A few seconds here, a few seconds there," says Gearhart. "It'll equal four minutes."

"I see. Are you a mathematician?" A smart-ass thing to say, but given my displeasure with this guy, well deserved.

"No." He says this matter-of-fact. "But maybe you should enjoy the journey."

Yeah, right. You and me. "What do you do?"

"Retired."

"From what."

"Government service."

Oh, shit. Could this be about jury duty? Or something worse? No way, I'm just being paranoid.

That's what happens when I go too long without a toke, another reason I need to get home.

Maybe the IRS?

I *never* declare tips.

I check out Gearhart in my rearview mirror—and he's checking *me* out.

Now I remember: He's been in the bar, when I was hosting karaoke. He didn't sing or anything, just sat quiet, watching.

Definitely the IRS.

Unless I'm under investigation for something bigger than tax evasion. (What's bigger than tax evasion?)

Or maybe he's an old homo. I've got nothing against gays—I even know a few—but it's not my scene.

"Tell me about yourself," he says.

I never should have taken this job.

"I live in Summerland," I say.

"You mean it's always summer for you?"

"Yeah, it is."

"Where are you from?"

"Stinson Beach, north of San Fran."

"Go on."

"I grew up in Bolinas, just up from Stinson, you know, but it's a weird place, full of old hippies who migrated from Haight-Ashbury, so I'll stick with Stinson Beach, where I learned to surf."

"What do your parents do?"

"Singular, dude. Just my mom. Never had a real dad."

In the early days, the commune, I had about *three* dads, but I didn't want to get into that, just like I didn't want to get into Bolinas. But what the hell, talking suddenly felt good.

"My mom grew up during the hippie era, you know. Free love. That's me, my life: the product of free love." *Like, now you satisfied?* "So tell me about *your* life."

Not that I was interested, just wanted to get off mine.

"I'm from the East Coast. Pennsylvania. I joined the army near the end of the Vietnam War and they sent me to Monterey for language training: French and Vietnamese. They were going to deploy me to Saigon to interrogate prisoners, but the war ended and I wound up in Washington, DC. I used the GI Bill to earn a master's in international relations at Georgetown University and joined the government. They sent me to Africa."

For a guy who'd hardly said boo the first six hours, this was quite the mouthful.

"Right on," I said, almost sorry I'd asked.

"Is that where you grew up, Stinson Beach?"

"Solvang. It's a Danish town in the valley."

"Bolinas didn't work out?"

This guy is actually listening. Better than my last two therapists.

"I think *hippie-dom* didn't work out. Solvang is where my mom was from. She ran away when she was sixteen, and ran back again so my grandparents could help bring me up. Solvang sucked for me, you know. No ocean, no waves, no surfing."

"Surfing is your sport?"

"Surfing isn't a sport, boss, it's a *lifestyle*."

"What else do you do?"

"What else *is* there?"

"To make a living, I mean."

"This." I grip the wheel. "And I have a karaoke gig at a bar. Uh, I did until last night."

"What happened last night?"

Nosy bastard. "No big deal."

"What do you *want* to do?"

"Well, since you asked: I'd like to get you where you're going, as soon as possible, and then get back to Summerland, as soon as possible."

"I understand that," says Gearhart. "But when I want whine, I open a bottle."

Funny guy!

"I get that. But it's my birthday today, you know. That's why . . ."

"Happy birthday."

"You think? I'm sitting behind this wheel all day."

"Aren't you enjoying the ride, the scenery?"

This stumps me. I actually hadn't noticed any scenery, just the road ahead.

"Aren't you getting hungry?" I ask. My mind won't let go of a billboard we passed offering all-you-can-eat Asian buffet for $6.99.

"I had a good breakfast. However, I just noticed that the clock has jumped an hour to Mountain Time, which means it is almost time for a cocktail. I suggest Cedar City, just up ahead."

4.

I fork right onto South Main for a sweep through this southern Utah town.

Being Mormon territory, there are only two bars, Toadz and Mike's Tavern. I sincerely doubt Gearhart would want a drink in either, which is fine by me, since the last thing I need is a drink on an empty stomach (my pretzels, long gone) or another DUI, which makes this just a time-waster.

Mike's, just off Main, is the easy find, and from the outside a typical dive.

Gearhart gets out of the car and buttons his blazer even though it's ninety-two degrees.

My mother had phoned earlier, so I tell him go ahead, I need to return a call.

He disappears inside and I have a mad impulse to hit the accelerator and barrel the hell out of there, leave Gearhart to his cocktail, to Cedar City, to the rest of his life. But I'd already screwed up my karaoke gig, and Santa Barbara is not the easiest place in the world to find work, especially without wheels.

So I call my mother, and she asks if I'm back yet, and I tell her *no, can you believe this? The guy I'm driving changed his mind and wants to go all the way to Utah instead.*

And all she has to say: call me when you get back, we'll celebrate my birthday with a lobster dinner at Fish Enterprise.

Which makes me hungrier than I already am, and I'm starving.

I lock Abe and go after Gearhart into Mike's Tavern, maybe hurry him up.

He's standing at the bar, trading small talk with local characters and a female barkeep with more tattoos than teeth, and sipping something transparent from a martini glass.

"Beefeater," he says to me. "Not my favorite, but it's all they have."

The inside is worse than the outside, dark and dingy, the opposite of the Biltmore where I'd picked him up, shit, nine hours ago—and we still have another three to reach Park City. Maybe the longest drive I've ever done in a day, in my life.

"Still in a hurry?" says Gearhart. "I never rush a martini."

When he finally finishes, the June sun is still bright in the sky—coming up on the longest day of the year.

"I think I'll sit up front," says Gearhart.

"Suit yourself." I'm happy just to get going.

I follow the one-way system and cut right onto N 100 West, double back toward Main.

Gearhart shakes his mane.

"Something wrong?"

"Tattoo parlors, pawn shops, abandoned shops . . . what has become of this country?"

"I guess you've never been to Oxnard. This is *nice*. Where've *you* been?"

"Overseas, mostly."

"Nicer over there?"

"I used to think of it as the Third World."

We rejoin I-15 after a wrong turn. Now my stomach is seriously pissed off.

"You wanna stop for something to eat?" I ask.

"Depends where."

"Subway's good, you know. You can usually find them at a Chevron station."

Not ten minutes later, an exit looms with signs for Chevron gas and Subway. I veer onto the ramp, right, and right again into their forecourt.

Gearhart alights, stretches, yawns, and ambles after me into Subway.

"I'm not eating here," he says.

"Why not?"

He raises and shakes his hands, by way of explanation, and turns on his heel, back to the car.

Truth be known, it truly is the scuzziest Subway I've ever seen, and I've seen a few. I follow him out.

"I'll wait till we arrive in Park City to eat," says Gearhart, re-immersing himself into his book.

5.

We reach Provo as the sun begins its final descent, late, but this is June *and* Mountain Time. We leave I-15 to its own destiny and take Route 189 all the way through this clean and wholesome town, past Brigham Young University, to mountains that yank us up a winding canyon road to over ten thousand feet.

The sun is setting by the time we reach Deer Creek Reservoir; a short dusk quickly morphs into a dark, moonless night. I keep going straight in Heber City on the wrong road until a sign sets me right.

By this time, we have been on the road for twelve hours, and I'm weary.

Finally: Park City. I pull into a space on the steep incline they call Main Street and consult my trip odometer: 793 miles. Unbelievable.

"What now, boss?" I cannot tell if he detects my sarcasm.

Gearhart presses a button to wind down his window, takes a good deep breath with his nose, and slowly exhales through his mouth. "Time for something to eat," he says.

I follow as he, on foot, conducts a quick inspection of eateries, up one side of the block, down the other, most of them closed. He stops at Riverhorse, consults a menu posted near the door, and nods. "This will do."

After ascending a staircase, he cuts right into the bar, asks a hostess if they serve the full menu there, they do, and he nails a high-top in the corner, back to the wall.

I'm ready to order everything on the menu and all he wants is a glass of their finest chardonnay, which he insists must be very cold and from a fresh bottle, opened not necessarily in front of him, but no earlier than today.

"When you pay fourteen dollars for a glass of wine," he says to me, "it ought not to be from yesterday. Would you eat yesterday's bread?"

He's asking the wrong guy, because right now I'd eat just about anything, including *last week's* bread, but I'll settle for a beer in deference to Gearhart, knowing my driving for the day is done, other than whatever short distance it takes to reach a hotel.

This is the subject Gearhart addresses with our server: a good place for an overnight stay.

She recommends the Marriott a mile down the road in Park City's modern commercial zone.

Next he tackles what to eat, asking her recommendations.

"What about the Riverhorse Burger?" I cut in.

"I wouldn't order that," she says.

And I've had just about enough of being told what to do and what not do all day long.

Gearhart settles on red trout.

"I'll have the Riverhorse Burger," I say.

He drains his white wine and orders a glass of red, their finest pinot noir, he says. *Fresh*.

"When you're traveling," he says to me, "you should stick to what's indigenous to the region. You can order a hamburger anywhere."

"I like hamburgers."

An air raid siren sounds. I jump up to see what it's about.

"Ten o'clock," explains the hostess. "An old miner's thing. Means everyone came up safe. I can hear it all the way where I live in Deer Valley, but right here we're at ground-zero."

"You know what this means?" I say to Gearhart, re-grabbing my bar stool.

He shrugs.

"If you have a buildup of intestinal gas, save it till 10:00 p.m. then let it rip as loud as you want."

He nods, sips his fresh glass of pinot noir. "You never really grew up, did you?"

"Why bother?"

To prove his point, and mine, I practically swallow the burger whole when it arrives.

"You always eat fast?" says Gearhart, barely starting his trout.

Only when I'm starving to death.

"You should take your time," he continues. "It's good manners. Chew. Savor each mouthful. You eat like you don't know where your next meal is coming from."

Yup, that's me.

When he's done, he puts his knife and fork down. "Well, I guess we should find a hotel. We have a long day tomorrow."

I know *I* do, driving twelve hours back to southern Cal, dammit. But I don't know why he's saying *we*.

Until he drops the bomb.

"Oh, didn't I mention?" says Gearhart. "We're heading north."

I'm too flabbergasted to say a thing, so he keeps jawboning.

"Big sky country," he continues.

"W-w-what?" I stammer. "Why?"

"I want to see what heaven looks like."

I'm shaking my head. "I'm not going north. I'm going home."

"Oh, didn't your company contact you? It's all arranged."

"No way." I'm still shaking my head. "Nobody has contacted me."

Nobody really had, even though it's my birthday.

"Well, I'm sure they will." Gearhart settles the tab and dismounts from his stool. "I guess we should find that hotel."

We roll down Main Street, curve right, and weave through a retail area, strip malls, into the Marriott's forecourt.

"I don't have a change of clothes," I think aloud. "I don't even have a toothbrush. Do they give you one in the hotel?"

"One what?"

"A toothbrush?"

Gearhart regards me with an amused expression. "We passed a CVS. Why don't you go back for toothpaste and a toothbrush, I'll get us a couple of rooms."

He gets out, goes in.

As I'm driving to CVS, I connect to The Drive Cycle. "*What the hell is going on?*"

"What do you mean?"

"My passenger says we're driving to big sky country tomorrow!"

"Oh, yeah, that's right. He called us. We've billed his card."

"I never signed on for this!"

"We don't have anyone to replace you with—you're too far away."

"I know I'm too friggin' far away! I've just spent the last twelve hours driving too friggin' far away!"

"Sorry, another call . . ." He disconnects me.

"That's it." I swing into the CVS lot, slam the brakes. *I'm outta here.*

And then I realize I'm not going anywhere. It's almost eleven, I'm dog-tired, and it's so dark outside I can barely find my way back to the Marriott.

A man awaits me with a key card and a room number. "Mister Gearhart has retired for the evening," he says. "He asked me to give you a key and requested you be ready for departure at 8:33."

"That's what he said—8:33?"

The receptionist double-checks his note. "Yes."

6.

For a few moments, upon awakening, I do not know where I am. It is still early, not quite seven, but daylight is streaming through my window, so I get up anyway, shower, turn my underwear inside out, and drive a couple blocks to a Starbucks. Then it's Abe's turn. I drive into Maverick's to quench his thirst. By now I am resigned to a second day with Charles Gearhart.

I position my wheels right outside the front door, trunk popped at exactly 8:33, and Gearhart appears on the dot, stows his garment bag, gently folds his blazer, and slides into the backseat.

"May I ask you a question, boss?"

"Shoot."

"Why 8:33 and not just 8:30?"

"When you're precise like that with the time people are more likely to be punctual."

"Got it. Next question: Where we headed now?"

"Wyoming. Jackson, Wyoming."

"Why?"

"To see the Grand Tetons—why else?"

I'm shaking my head, because hell if I know *why else*. I check the routing on my smartphone: a brief stint on I-80 West, turn north on 189, a trunk road.

"Did you leave a tip for the maid?" asks Gearhart.

"Uh, was I supposed to?"

"When was the last time you stayed in a hotel?"

"I don't remember?"

"Think back. How long?"

"Three or four years. Marina Del Rey." I pause. "She paid."

"It's customary to leave a buck or two. Sleep well?"

"I did the fitness room for a few minutes and couldn't sleep because I was short of breath, you know, and I thought, oh my God, I'm having a heart attack. But then I realized I'm acclimatizing to ten thousand feet up."

"No," says Gearhart. "That was the Riverhorse Burger our waitress advised you against."

For the first hour, Gearhart is lost in a new stack of newspapers: *USA Today* and the *Salt Lake Tribune* and whatever else. He finally perks up when we enter Wyoming, and stirs when we come upon Kemmerer: POPULATION 2651, ELEVATION 692—says the welcome sign.

Oddly, there are five or six motels on both sides of the road of this small town as we enter.

"Who would vacation here?" I ask, the first sound I've made since leaving Utah.

"I used to," says Gearhart softly.

"Really?"

"Yes."

"Why?"

"My grandparents lived here. Born and bred. When I was a kid we used to come every summer to see them." He twists his neck this way and that. "Hasn't changed much."

Route 189 turns into Main Street, with a town triangle instead of a square, a few bars.

Gearhart smiles. "Still here."

"The town?"

"No. J. C. Penney. That's their very first store, opened in 1902." A yellow sign says J. C. PENNEY COMPANY, and the street sign says J. C. PENNEY DRIVE. "Pull over, let's go in."

"Why?

"You need supplies."

"From J. C. Penney's?"

Gearhart shrugs. "Where else around here?"

He enters and strolls the aisles, marveling at what he sees around him, turns to me. "They still do a St. John's Bay line. Probably made in China these days."

He inspects a tag. "Yep. I still have a CPO jacket from here, St. John's Bay, but made in the USA—I've worn it longer than anything I own." He stops in the shirt section, picks up a white button-down—two or more for $19.99. "What size are you?"

"Sixteen-and-a-half."

"Here, take three of these."

Next: chinos.

Specifically, St. John's Bay Worry Free Slider Relaxed Fit Flat-Front at $24.99 a pair.

"Size?" says Gearhart.

"Thirty-four waist."

He hands me two pairs.

"How about a sport coat?"

"Must I?"

"Jackson is a nice place."

"As long as it's not a navy blazer with brass buttons."

"Try this on." Gearhart hands me a khaki linen sport coat, on sale for $100.

I put it on.

"Button the top button and turn around," says Gearhart.

I can't believe I actually comply.

"Perfect," he says. "Now, go choose your own underwear."

Gee, thanks.

We regroup a couple minutes later.

"One last thing," says Gearhart. "Shoes."

"Who's paying for all this stuff?"

Gearhart shrugs. "Me. I'm the one who took you on an overnight road trip without warning. Consider it part of your compensation."

"I'd rather have the money."

"In that case, it's a present."

"Can I have a pair of sneakers?"

"No. Here's what I'm gifting you."

"Florsheim penny loafers? You must be kidding. I need my feet for surfing."

"After wearing them a few months they'll be the most comfortable shoes you've ever owned."

The *only* shoes I've ever owned.

I'm sure the sales lady, who might have been there since they opened in 1902, thought we were gay, probably staying at the pink Chateau Motel up the road.

Throw in three pairs of socks—not that I intended to wear them—and the tab comes to just over $350.

Gearhart nails it with a credit card.

"Next," he says, "a bathroom kit."

Jubilee Pharmacy is just around the corner on Pine Street.

"Just load up on whatever you need," he says. "I recommend deodorant."

"Huh?"

"Meet me at the cash register."

I use this opportunity to check in with my mom, tell her I'm in Wyoming and that my passenger is buying me stuff to wear since I didn't know I'd be away a few days, is that okay?

It makes sense, she says, because I didn't have a chance to pack my own things. "When will you be back?" she asks.

"That's what I'd like to know. At least another day. You think I should cut this fare loose?"

"You're getting paid, and you're getting away from your comfort zone. Maybe you should just enjoy the ride?"

"Yeah, that's what my fare says. Gotta go."

I grab a pack of Bic razors and Gillette foam and roll-on deodorant and bring it to the front.

"Ever have a real shave?" says Gearhart.

"Yeah, I don't use electric."

"Put the foam back. Grab some real shaving soap and the finest brush they have. And put these Bics back, too. Here's what you need." He holds up a fancy Fusion razor. "You have to take *joy* in shaving."

"I don't see anything joyful about shaving."

"Then you're not living your life properly," says Gearhart. "You've got to take joy in all the little things, not look at them as chores, delight in them."

"In a shave?"

"In many things. But *especially* a shave."

I glance at the antique sales lady, roll my eyes. "If you say so."

Outside, Gearhart sniffs the air. "Smells the same." He seems to lose himself in time. "It's amazing the memories an aroma can induce. Smell is the most underrated of senses."

7.

South of Le Barge, we drive past an old diner called Moondance, deserted and boarded up.

"I read about that place in the newspaper," Gearhart pipes up. "They moved it from New York City. I guess it didn't work out."

North of Le Barge, I hit Abe hard, one of my *bursts*, and then I slow him down to overtake an SUV.

"I think you just overtook a cop," says Gearhart with a smirk on his face.

"Really? What makes you think so?"

"The word SHERIFF stenciled on the side."

At that moment, police lights begin flashing behind me. "You think he's after someone else?"

"Who?" says Gearhart. "There's no one else on the road. I guess he wants to thank you for showing him respect by slowing down to overtake him."

Smart-ass.

I pull over.

The guardian of the law gets out, saunters over. "Where is it you're going so fast?"

"Uh, Jackson, officer."

He regards Abe. "Figures. I clocked you going eighty-one."

"Isn't this a seventy-mile-an-hour road?" I say.

"You're talking about the interstate. This is the highway. Sixty-five miles an hour. And you were going eighty-one."

"I'm very careful driving through towns and passing other cars, you know. Can't you let me off with a warning, officer?"

He shakes his head. "Not when you're goin' eighty-one. I can give you a break and write it up as seventy-nine, help you with your insurance company. License and registration." He returns to his vehicle with my docs.

"It was bound to happen," says Gearhart from behind me. "All your talk about *bursts*."

"I can't believe this. I'm gonna get fired. And I'll have to enroll in their stupid online driver's-ed program. And I'll have to pay a huge fine. I'm totally screwed."

"If you don't like the consequences, why take the risk? To get to Jackson five minutes earlier?"

"We would've made better time than that."

"I doubt it. But even if we did, so what?"

I shake my head, totally disgusted by getting a ticket, by being in Wyoming, by having a smart-ass passenger dumping on my driving skills.

"Hello, officer." Gearhart addresses the bacon through my lowered window when he returns with a pad and pen. "My driver got a little too used to the high speed limit in Utah. But I've got an idea."

"Who are *you*?"

"My name is Charles Gearhart, and this road trip is my project, not his. Tell you what, I'll change places with him and drive this car myself—his punishment for going too fast."

"I don't know—he was going eighty-one."

Gearhart never takes his eyes out of the bacon's. "And when he's back in the driver's seat, I'll personally make sure he sticks to the speed limit."

Something happens, and I still haven't figured out what Gearhart did. But the sheriff's deputy puts his ticket pad back into in his pocket and says, "Just make sure he doesn't drive again till you're clear out of Wyoming."

Gearhart holds his gaze. "You've got my word." He opens his door, climbs out, and stands next to mine. "And you have Luke's word, too. Right, Luke?"

Like, I don't have any say in this?

"Right, boss."

As the bacon retreats, I shake my head in disgust, muttering, "I don't friggin' believe this." But I get out, walk around the front, and get into the passenger seat next to Gearhart, who adjusts the driver's seat and mirrors to his own specs, winces in pain briefly, then eases onto the road.

"You know," says Gearhart, turning to look at me. "You have a *you know* problem."

"*Excuse me?*"

"Half the time you say something, you say *you know*, but by almost getting a ticket you proved you actually don't know shit."

"I'm supposed to sit here and be insulted *and* let you drive?"

"You have no choice," says Gearhart. "I gave my word. You did, too. A man is nothing without his word."

"My fingers were crossed. How did you *do* that, anyway?"

"Do what?"

"Get Mr. Authority Figure, oink-oink, to cut me some slack."

Gearhart shrugs. "Just looked in his eyes. He used discretion, which is very rare these days in law enforcement, rare anywhere for that matter. Their penalties are based on collecting revenues. The point is, he made you a deal, he did you a favor, and now you've got to stick to your end of the bargain."

"Hell, he's going to turn around and drive back to Le Barge," I say.

"You're going to stick to your word for *you*, not for him."

"Or what?"

"Or you'll never have any self-respect. And, by the way, you're the first person I ever met who got a speeding ticket from a cop who was driving in *front* rather than behind."

In the distance, serious thunderheads grab my attention. "That's some storm ahead."

"Cumulonimbus," says Gearhart. "Beautiful."

"What's so beautiful about rain?"

"It washes all the crap away." He sets the wipers in action to clear the first sprinkles of rain, and with it a smattering of squished bugs. "See?"

A bolt of lightning cracks from sky to ground, dead ahead of us.

"Whoa!" I say. "Did you see that?"

"We're going smack into the center of the storm," says Gearhart, with the most enthusiasm I'd seen him muster since we left the Biltmore in Montecito.

"I'm not sure about this."

"About what?"

"We could die!"

"You can't be serious," says Gearhart. "You're frightened of a little rain?"

"Not the rain. The lightning!"

At that moment, an enormous bolt strikes the road ahead of us, impacting with a flash of orange— BOOM!

"See! We could die! I should drive!"

"Relax. Lightning is much safer than artillery shells."

"Artillery shells?"

"I've driven in places where incoming is *targeted*, not random. I think I can get us through a thunderstorm."

"What were you doing in places like that?"

"My job."

A deluge like no other I've ever experienced consumes Abe, pummels him, as more lightning crashes around us. I curl up, hands over my ears, waiting for it to pass—storms always frightened me as a kid— but it goes on and on and on until I close it out with a brief snooze.

8.

On the other side of the storm, mountains dusted with snow appear, and nature glistens beneath moody clouds.

"You survived," says Gearhart, eyes on the road. "Congratulations."

"Where are we?"

"Not far from our destination." He points at an upcoming sign to Jackson, only twelve miles away.

"Is that your final destination?"

"Everyone has the same final destination," says Gearhart. "That's why you have to enjoy the journey."

"Where is this journey taking us?"

"After Jackson? Told you already: big sky country. Montana."

He's serious.

Not ten minutes later we pull into Jackson. First the modern part, then the historic town, bustling with tourists.

Cowboy and Indian heaven.

"They truly are astonishing," says Gearhart, craning his neck to look up.

"What?"

"The Grand Tetons. French for tits."

"Now you're talking my language."

"For once, the French got it right. They are magnificent. Now, a place to stay . . . right there." He points left, up North Glenwood Street. "That's the one I've read about. The Wort Hotel." He pulls over on West Broadway. "Stay with the car, I'll see if they have rooms."

And I'm sitting here, thinking, *what the hell am I doing in Jackson, Wyoming?*

Five minutes later, Gearhart returns. "They just have one room. You have to sleep in the car."

"What?"

It wouldn't be the first time.

"Just kidding. They had just two rooms left. It's a nice place. Good thing you have something decent to wear."

Another ten minutes and I key myself into maybe the coolest room I've ever had to myself: Western décor, comfortable bed, and a clean, modern bathroom.

Unlike the marathon drive of the day before, I have a couple hours to relax and I finally think to Google *Charles Gearhart*, see who the hell he is.

I do this in the Wort's business center. Eighty-seven of them in Whitepages. I go to Images. Nothing matches my passenger. So I add *US Government* to his name. Zippo.

Gearhart said I should do whatever I wanted the rest of the afternoon and evening, but that he would be at the Wort's Silver Dollar Bar at 5:33 precisely and I should feel welcome to join him for a cocktail.

He is sitting there—last stool, far end of the bar—when I arrive, a martini before him.

I'm sporting my new threads: white button-down, chinos, sport coat, and loafers.

Gearhart rubs his eyes for a second look, smiles. "I almost didn't recognize you. Looks like you finally grew up."

I shake my head. "That's not possible."

"Would you like a real drink?"

"You mean a shot?"

"No. Only people who want to get drunk drink shots. The key to smart drinking is the opposite: turn a strong libation into a long one, never get drunk."

"What's the point?"

"You drink to relax your faculties, not lose them."

"How does that work?"

"Bartender?" Gearhart calls out. "Another just like mine." He turns to me. "Hendrick's gin, barely a dash of vermouth, lemon twist—and I make him leave the shaker."

"Why?"

"I stir it around, pour it myself, a little at a time. One, it keeps the gin nice and cold; two, it gives the ice time to melt and dilute the gin with water. In ten minutes my glass will still be full. The other way, shake and pour? It's like injecting alcohol directly into a vein."

The barkeep sets a martini glass and shaker on the bar in front of me.

"It's about the ritual," says Gearhart. "You always need the right accoutrements, whether you're shaving or drinking a martini."

I swirl the shaker, pour a little liquid crystal into my glass.

"Start by touching your lips with it, go slow," says Gearhart. "Taste the juniper." He does this himself. "The only thing as good as a well-made martini is a fine cigar." He consults the bartender about a smoke shop in town. "There's no crisis that can't be solved with a martini and a cigar."

"What if the IRS is after you?"

"Martini and a cigar."

"What if you've got cancer?"

Gearhart considers this. "A martini and a cigar. And it's a damn shame I can't smoke one in this bar."

He goes through the motions with a pretend cigar, the most animated I've seen him. "So, what are you missing by being here?"

"Surfing. Some people surf the *Net* all day and all night. I keep it real. There's nothing more real than getting axed."

"Axed?"

"A heavy wipeout."

"No ambition to do anything else?"

"Not really."

"Why not?"

"Why bother?"

"Self-respect, change the world."

"Look, I grew up with three dads in a commune, they taught me to enjoy nature, and in Bolinas that meant the beach and the ocean. They all believed in peace and love, but by the time my mother and I left, everyone was squabbling with everyone else over everything, and they were suspicious of outsiders, to a point where they hated anyone new who showed up in town. They went from flower power to paranoia. Do you know to this day there are no road signs to Bolinas? You know why? Every time Caltrans puts up a new sign, a bunch of old hippies—the self-proclaimed Bolinas Border Patrol—take it down. They think the whole town belongs to them—and they don't want visitors. When I moved to Solvang, no dad, just a granddad who thought he was still in Denmark. So I found my own way."

"You ever think of getting married?"

"Once. Almost got engaged ten years ago. She wanted commitment, but I came to my senses. Anyway, why are you so interested? Why did you ask for *me* to drive you here?"

"I didn't ask for you."

"That's what dispatch told me."

Gearhart looks me straight in the eye. "Maybe they didn't have anyone else. I've booked dinner around the corner at a place called Locals. Do join us."

Us?

Truth be known, I'm short on cash, hungry, and wherever I go with Gearhart, he pays, as he should, since I'm here sort of against my will, and he gets that.

"Unless, of course, you have other plans," he says patronizingly.

"I could probably swing it," I say.

Gearhart glances at his vintage wristwatch. "I have just enough time to pick up a cigar." He swigs the last drop of his drink. "Locals is next door to the famous Cowboy Bar, around the corner from here. Enjoy the rest of your drink and I'll meet you there in ten minutes."

9.

When I arrive, Gearhart—cagey bastard—is sitting with an attractive young woman who I guess is in her early thirties. She has long reddish-brown hair, a fair complexion, a smattering of freckles, and full lips, the natural kind, not the sort you find at bars in Montecito, between Summerland and Santa Barbara. Such natural poise and sophistication—the thought pops in my mind that Gearhart must have hired her from a local escort agency. After all, he could have rented a car and driven himself to Wyoming, so I'm guessing he's lonely, needs company.

They are side by side, backs to the wall, a table for four, with a bottle of red wine and three glasses.

Gearhart rises and beckons me to sit across from the babe.

"This is Katharine," he says.

A waiter is quickly upon me.

"What's indigenous?" I ask, looking between him and Gearhart.

"Everyone loves our Buffalo Tartare," says the waiter.

"See what I mean?" Katharine says to Gearhart.

"Let's share a portion," Gearhart instructs the waiter, "see what it's like." Then he turns to me. "Katharine is an artist. She was just telling me that though things have gotten better economically since the financial crash of 2008, most people who come here tend to buy things that have a buffalo on it, like whiskey glasses, instead of fine art."

"So why don't you paint buffalo?" I say to her.

"My specialty is nocturnes," she says. "I like the color of the night, its mood and mysteries."

"Easy," I reply. "Paint buffalos at night."

Gearhart chuckles.

"Maybe I'll try that," she says.

"Right on. Are you from around here?"

"Not originally, but I've been here a while."

"Where from?"

"I was born in Paris, and I grew up in Washington, DC. I came out here to paint one summer and never left."

"Nice. Can you make a living as an artist?" Part of my problem is I have zero understanding of boundaries.

Katharine chuckles. "Probably not. That's why I run an art gallery here in town, the Gearhart Gallery."

I look at Gearhart, then at Katharine, then back at Gearhart. "Are you two related?"

"Katharine is my daughter."

"Oh." I didn't know what else to say.

"Would you like a glass of wine?" asks Gearhart.

"I'm not a wine person, maybe I'll have a beer." Truth be known, the only wine I've ever drunk is Gallo by the jug, which I once got sick on, or Sutter Home miniatures, which split my skull the next morning.

"Maybe you haven't had fine wine? This is pinot noir from the Willamette Valley in Oregon." He pours a little into the third glass. "Try a little."

I sip and swallow. "I like green eggs and ham, Sam-I-Am!"

When the Buffalo Tartare arrives it takes all my strength not to wage war over it with Gearhart and daughter.

"So you're his daughter," I say, pointing my finger back and forth between them. "Is there a wife-slash-mother somewhere?"

Gearhart looks down, forks a bite of tartare.

"My mother passed a few years ago," Katharine says quietly, studying me, a gaze I turn away from.

"I'm sorry, I didn't mean . . ."

"No," she says, "it's okay. She went into the hospital for some minor surgery and ended up catching a blood infection, MRSA. It happened just like that, very unexpected."

"Any sisters or brothers?"

Katharine shakes her head. "My father tells me you're his driver for a few days."

I nod. "That's what I do. The Drive Cycle. When I'm not surfing."

Our server looms. "How is the tartare?"

Its total absence speaks for itself.

Gearhart orders sautéed Idaho trout all round, and it is not only indigenous, but the finest fish I've eaten in my whole life—though their Chef Burger on the next table never stops speaking to me.

After I devour mine, which doesn't take long, Gearhart says, "I'm glad you could join us, Luke, but if you don't mind, I'd like to finish up with my daughter. A little private time."

"Of course." I practically jump up, and out, cross North Cache Street, and wander into Jackson's town square with its elk-antler arches at each corner, stopping at a bench to take off my new loafers, rub my aching feet. How could anybody *wear* such things?

I'm still sitting there, enjoying the night, when they come out of Locals.

Katharine hugs Gearhart, real close, real long. Looks like she doesn't want to let go. Makes me wish, for a few seconds anyway, I had someone to hug like that.

Gearhart stands there in front of the restaurant, watches her turn a corner. Then he walks to the corner himself, crosses over to the square, nails a bench, and lights a cigar.

I wait a few minutes before getting up to approach him. "Sorry, taking a walk, saw you here."

"That's fine, sit down," says Gearhart. "Try a Macanudo."

"Sure."

I put it in my mouth, light 'er up, inhale, and cough it out . . .

"You don't inhale a cigar."

"Habit."

"Let the smoke roll around your mouth, blow it out."

"Your daughter is nice."

"Yes, she is. Thank you."

"Is it okay if I ask for her number?"

Gearhart chuckles. "Sure."

"Really?"

"I said yes."

I take another drag and try to stop myself inhaling. "Do you have any idea where we're driving tomorrow?"

"Montana."

"Where in Montana?"

"We'll see when we get there."

"You knew you were coming *here*, though, to see your daughter, right?"

"I certainly had it in my mind."

"Why didn't you say so, instead of Vegas?"

"I didn't have a plan. Vegas sounded good. But I didn't like the look of it. I just wanted a road trip." He pauses. "You know, Luke, I'm happy for you to keep driving me. But if you have pressing business back home, or you just don't feel like driving any farther, I'll release you and rent a car."

"Really? Can I think about it?"

"Sure. Decide in the morning."

"If I decide to keep going, can *I* drive tomorrow?"

"Of course." He pauses, winks. "Once we're out of Wyoming. Remember, a deal's a deal. And another thing: once the cigar burns down to the size of your thumb, stub it out."

10.

As much as I like my Wort room, and how comfort-able the bed is, I toss and turn all night, dreaming wildly, nothing I can remember except the last dream before I wake up, where I'm a little kid and I'm sit-ting at my own birthday party, nobody but me, with a small party hat on my head and a cake with blue icing and candles, and that Eric Carmen song "All by Myself" playing in the background.

It gets me up early in a cold sweat, and across the road to Jackson Hole Coffee Roasters.

I'd decided to cut out, get back to the waves, the beach bunnies, my stash, my life . . .

I'm thinking maybe I'll just leave, write *good-bye* to Gearhart in a note I'd leave at reception.

Then my mother calls as I'm finishing the last of my coffee. I tell her I'm heading back. She asks the situation, and I explain it to her.

And she says, "I saw something yesterday on Facebook that may apply . . ."

Old hippies don't fade away, I feel like saying, *they get hooked on Facebook and all the slogans people post.*

"A Mark Twain quote," she continues: "*Explore. Dream. Discover.*"

"All the way to Montana?"

"If you're in Jackson, you're only a few hours from Montana."

"Oh."

I'm still minded to split.

But Charles Gearhart surfaces before I get it together to write a letter and, seeing him, I impulsively decide to continue the journey for another day, I rationalize, after which I'll reassess.

"Sleep well?" Gearhart asks.

"No."

"Why not?"

"Don't know."

Now *he's* chirpy and *I'm* aloof.

Gearhart opts for Route 22, which quickly puts us into Idaho. True to word, he pulls over in a town called Driggs—a life-size buffalo on the roof of a building—and lets me back behind the wheel.

"Your daughter's right," I say. "Up here, it's all about buffalo."

"It's hard to go wrong in Jackson," he says, clipping his seatbelt up front next to me. "Tourism means revenue. If you're not going to live in a big city to make a living, live and work where the big cities *come to you*. They go where the relics are."

"Relics?"

"Hundreds and hundreds of years ago, tourism was based around relics. A town needed something that would draw pilgrims seeking relief from health issues or as a way of expressing their faith. Relics were the bones of saints or martyrs or famed holy people. It was thought their bones had special powers—to cure disease or restore faith. This led to *skullduggery*. Holy robbers from one town would steal relics from another, bring them back, claim ownership, and put them on display to draw pilgrims, and more importantly their money.

"It takes other forms today. Lenin's Mausoleum in Moscow. And in Italy, hundreds of thousands of people visit San Giovanni Rotondo to see the preserved body of St. Pio. It's about the revenue."

"That's cynical," I say.

"I once knew a reporter in Paris, dead now, but he was an American jazz critic for the *Trib*. His finest writing, however, was for an English-language magazine that didn't last long. He had a great pseudonym: Johnny Staccato. And a great column called 'Reality is Money.'" Gearhart pauses. "What books are you reading?"

"Right now, nothing."

"What was the last book you read?"

I suppose I could have made something up, but why bother? "I don't remember." Almost in defense of myself, I add, "Who reads books anymore?"

"Smart people."

"So you're saying I'm not smart?"

"Maybe you are. But you're not smart as you could be if you're not reading books. Just because you think no one reads anymore doesn't mean you can't. And if what you're saying is true, and *you* read books, you'll be one of the smartest people around."

I consider this argument. "But it's not cool to be smart anymore."

"Not cool?"

"No. Haven't you gone to the movies, or watched TV? Dumb is cool, dumber is cooler."

Gearhart shakes his head in dismay, but brightens when he looks up to see a giant rotating mug of root beer that greets us at a key intersection in Ashton.

"You don't see much Americana like this anymore," says Gearhart.

"Let's stop and grab a bite to eat."

Gearhart scowls at me. "I meant it was interesting to *look* at, not to *eat* in."

When the light turns green I zip straight into Frostop's parking zone and kill the ignition. "I'm going in whether you're coming or not."

I get out, leave Gearhart in the car, take a stool at the old-fashioned lunch counter, and consult a menu. Free-radical heaven—my kind of grub.

A minute later, I feel a presence at my side. It's him, gingerly handling a menu.

"What do you recommend?" he asks.

"I'm having a grilled cheese and ham sandwich, tater tots, and a root beer."

A server overhears, takes it down.

"I guess I'll have the same," he says reluctantly.

And damn if he doesn't scarf down every last morsel, including all the greasy tater tots.

"I'm not going to say it was as good as what we ate last night," I say, after a final gulp of root beer. "But you have to admit, this was pretty damn tasty."

"Not bad," he sniffs. "Maybe we should share a piece of pie?"

Either a sugar high or the root beer—which he says he hasn't drunk in half a century—makes Gearhart giddy with happiness.

Buttered and battered, we rejoin Abe.

"How old are you?" I ask, climbing behind the wheel.

"Sixty-three."

A few moments later, just past the Ashton Visitors Center on the outskirts of town, we see up ahead a lone male by the road, his thumb pointing in our direction.

"Let's pick him up," says Gearhart.

"You're kidding, right?"

"No, I'm serious. Let's give him a ride, learn something new."

"Like what?"

"We'll see," says Gearhart. "Everyone knows something we don't."

"I bet we don't learn a damn thing, other than he smells bad."

"If that's what it takes, I'll give you two-to-one odds. My ten bucks to your five."

I swerve over, fifty yards ahead of the hitchhiker.

"I could get in a lot of trouble for this," I say. "Company policy strictly prohibits picking up hitch-hikers."

"I'm not telling."

I see him trudging toward us in my rearview mirror. Slim, about five foot eight, long brown and sun-bleached unkempt hair way beyond his shoulders, long V-shaped beard, checkered short sleeve green shirt buttoned to the top, tails hanging over blue jeans rolled up his calves, and thongs on his feet, carrying a green duffel, probably army surplus.

He opens the back door, slides in. "Thank you," he says. "I'm tired."

I can smell him already as I turn and study his face: hollow cheeks, intense green eyes.

"Where you going?" I ask.

"Canada."

"We can get you to Montana. Why are you going to Canada?"

"I don't like this country anymore."

"Why not?"

"Too bossy. To the world. But especially to Americans."

"What's your name?" says Gearhart.

"Bart."

"So, Bart." Gearhart seems to be enjoying himself. "You must be the opposite of a Mexican."

"I think this country was at its best when it welcomed the sick and the poor and the oppressed from everywhere else. All this immigration nonsense is just a sideshow, like most party politics, to distract from the real issues. That's what they do whenever people unite to ask some serious questions. They turn it into a race or gender issue and divide everyone until they get bored and go back to sports and movies."

"They?"

"The folks who are really in charge. They privatize the gain, socialize the loss, and steal everyone's money. There's a machine in motion, like a huge locomotive, it goes 150 miles an hour and can't be stopped. No point telling anyone, no one will believe you anyway, and if they do, and you gain any following, they'll call you a crank and get the mainstream media to ridicule you, or create far-fetched theories of their own to distract and muddy the water. Man, I don't want to talk about what's really going on, you'll probably throw me out of your car and I just want to get to Canada."

"You think it's different up there?" asks Gearhart.

Bart ponders this. "I don't rightly know. But I know this country isn't as free as they pretend it is. I'm guessing the fewer the people around, the more freedom." He leans forward. "Your engine light is on."

"Yeah, it happens on and off," I say. "Usually a computer glitch, but the manual says nothing serious, it can wait."

"I don't know, man," says Bart. "I wouldn't trust it."

"Honest Abe?"

"There's a gas station coming up in Island Park. I'd pull in if I was you."

Now I'm really sorry I picked up this trouble-making know-it-all. But it's rural out here, and Abe is down to a quarter-tank, so why not fill 'er up.

"There it is." Bart points to Elk Creek Station on the right.

I pull aside a gas pump, climb out, feed Abe.

Before I know it, Bart's got the hood open and he's wiping the oil gauge, dipping it back in. He rubs his beard and goes for a second dip, looking at me, an astonished expression. "You're out of oil."

"What?"

"When was the last time you checked it?"

I shrug. *Who checks oil? That's what the service department is for.*

He goes into the shop, returns with two quarts.

Gearhart is observing everything through his open window.

Bart pours a whole quart, stands by about ninety seconds and then re-dips the stick. "What the . . . ?" He bends down, looks under the car. "*That's* not good." He looks up at me. "Man, you got a major leak. The oil's pouring out of there!"

"Where?" I follow his finger and see black liquid pooling on the ground, as if poor Abe is bleeding.

"O-M-G! Should I drive it over to the mechanic's garage?"

"No way, man. Don't even start the engine, it might crack. Hold on." Bart trots off to the garage, returns with a flat board on wheels, rolls himself face up beneath Abe, twists and turns. After about a minute he resurfaces. "It's your lucky day, man. Loose oil filter. I tightened it. If you'd needed a pan, you might have been stuck here a few days to order parts. And if you'd kept driving . . ."—he shakes his head— ". . . you would have needed a whole new engine. But we're not out of this yet, let's see what happens." Bart pours another quart of oil, then gets down on all fours to watch for dripping. "So far so good." He waits, tests the gauge. "Getting better." He goes back inside the shop, buys another quart, drains it, waits, tests again, nods. "Yep, your lucky day. We're good to go."

Gearhart is watching me, smirking.

I go pay for engine oil, the best $71.41 I ever spent.

Posted on the wall, Elk Creek Station's creed:

> *Life's journey is not to arrive*
> *at the grave safely*
> *in a well preserved body,*
> *but rather to slide in sideways,*
> *worn out and shouting*
> *"Holy shit, what a ride!"*

I rejoin Gearhart and Bart in the car and pull off.

"That could have been catastrophic," says Gearhart, "but it got resolved without hoopla or much money. Well done, Bart. How old are you?"

"Thirty-three."

"Where did you learn about cars?"

"I got raised on a farm. Tractors, mostly. Woulda stayed there, but my family lost it."

"How?"

"New government regulations on how we could farm and how we couldn't. Next thing, my dad died and inheritance tax nailed us. Government's taking over everything, one way or another."

"You think Canada is the answer?"

"I don't have the answer, man. I'm looking for it. What are *you* looking for?"

"Right on, Bart," I say, "that's what *I'd* like to know."

Gearhart shrugs in that whimsical way of his, looking out the window. "The only way to understand something is to see it up close," he finally replies. "Right now I'm trying to understand my country."

"But why with me?" I ask, reinforced by Bart.

Gearhart turns in my direction. "You know what Clint Eastwood says to actors who ask him what their motivation is supposed to be in the roles they're playing in movies he directs?"

Bart and I exchange puzzled glances through my rearview mirror.

"No, what?" I ask.

"He says, your paycheck."

"That's it?"

"It," says Gearhart. "I want to see my country, and you're getting paid to drive me."

11.

Route 20 takes a sharp right into Montana, through West Yellowstone, and back into Wyoming, where it hugs the border for a stretch.

Gearhart sees the sign like he sees everything, even when he's reading.

"Do we need to change places?" I ask.

He shakes his mane. "The business I was in, rules were made to be broken."

"What business?"

"Uncle Sam."

Bart finally comes to from the backseat. "You work for the government?"

"Retired."

"Who killed Kennedy?"

Gearhart chuckles sourly. "Which one?"

"Both of them, but I meant JFK."

"Does it matter anymore?"

"Matters to me."

"Why?"

"That was the day—November 22, 1963—this country started its steep decline."

Gearhart shifts, takes one of his deep nose breaths. "Can't argue with that."

"So do you know?"

Gearhart chuckles sourly. "I was too busy doing what I was doing to delve into anything like that. What I found, generally, is that there's *less* to most things than meets the eye."

Bart nods his head vigorously in my rearview mirror. "That's right," he says. "That's where the magician's sleight of hand lives. They ruse us with the *more*, so we don't look at the *less*."

"Route 191 North is certainly the road *less* traveled," I say, weary of this dialogue. For me, the truth exists in the Pope's Living Room, which is to say, inside the curl of a breaking wave. "There's nobody on it but us. And we just crossed back into Montana. Look." I point to a sign that says BIG SKY, 18 MILES. "It exists as a real place." Turns out it's not a town, just a resort. "So we're here," I say to Gearhart. "Big Sky, Montana. What now?"

"We need an overnight. Let's drive on to Bozeman and see what it's like, and then on to Livingston, twenty miles east. I've been told that's the *real* Montana."

Route 191 leads us smack through the center of Bozeman.

Bart bails on West Main Street in front of the Lewis and Clark Motel's grand marquee.

I don't think Livingston is so bad, just quiet. But Gearhart seems disheartened.

"*This* is the real Montana?" he says more than once as we circle around for the full experience. "I'm not staying in this rinky-dink town."

"We can double back to Bozeman," I offer.

"I'm not staying there, either. I wouldn't see why."

"Maybe run into Bart. I kind of miss him."

"You ought to," says Gearhart. "He saved your ass. I need to see a map." Gearhart turns and leans into the backseat, rummages around in his satchel. "Butte," he says after surveying the situation. "It's not too far, maybe an hour."

Not far is important at this juncture, because it is now around 4:30 and I'm accustomed to Gearhart's rituals, namely, cocktail hour at 5:33.

Butte looks appealing as we approach, set on a hill next to another range of hills stripped bare—all orange and raw from copper mining.

We ascend the hill in search of this city's downtown historic district and soon discover it has not been renovated and re-gentrified like historic downtowns elsewhere.

"How depressing." Gearhart shakes his mane with disdain. "This was one of the richest towns in America. Anaconda copper. Is that how they thank it for providing so much?"

We cruise past pawnshops, tattoo parlors, consignment shops, and discount nail salons; abandoned buildings and decrepit dive bars; decay and dilapidation.

"There's supposed to be a famous old hotel around here." Gearhart cranes his neck. "The Finlen."

We find it, on a street that could be nicknamed *Desolation Row*. If there's any activity at all, and there isn't, it's in the Finlen's motor inn, adjacent to the once grand hotel.

"I'll be damned," says Gearhart. "There must be a newer part of town. Let's find it."

The newer part of town turns out to be an area near the airport, where Route 393 and I-15 intersect and motels like Best Western and fast-food shacks like Wendy's fill out an assortment of strip malls.

This bothers Gearhart even more than the pawnshops and tattoo parlors of old town.

"Dear, oh dear," he despairs. "What has American culture become? The moneymakers rape a lovely town of its natural resources and leave behind shoebox rooms and processed food. Makes me think the American dream has transformed into a nightmare."

It is now nearing 7:00 p.m.

"We could stay at the Best Western," I suggest.

It looks fine to me. The only other high-end hotel, the Copper King, is boarded up, chained off, and abandoned.

"I'm not staying here. Makes me think humanity is a cancerous tumor trying to kill Mother Nature, and that's not why I came here, not what I want to see, think about, or know."

I only later discovered that Gearhart was more right than he knew: The Berkeley Pit, where Anaconda mined minerals, is reputed to be the most toxic place on earth.

"Let's at least get Abe fed."

I pull into a service station in the middle of Gearhart's definition of hell and I pump gas while Gearhart studies his map, muttering, "Options, options."

I climb back in.

"Okay, I've figured it out," says Gearhart. "The right place to stay in Montana is not in a town or a city, but at a resort. There must be one within an hour of here."

I pop *resorts near Butte* into my smartphone.

It responds with *Fairmont Hot Springs Resort*.

I click into it: twenty miles west of Butte.

"Yes, let's go there," says Gearhart.

A dog suddenly barks from somewhere so close, it scares the living crap out of me. I turn around and come head-to-head with a Chihuahua—though it could be part weasel and part bat—and maybe, with white face and black markings around the eyes, part raccoon.

"What the . . . !"

Incredulous, Gearhart turns to see what I see.

"How the hell did a dog get in here?"

Gearhart has it figured. "Bart."

"Bart?"

"He must have had it with him."

"What do we do with it?"

Gearhart shakes his head, already discombobulated by our circumstances.

"We can drive back to Butte, try to find Bart."

"You can if you want. First take me to the resort."

We practically fly to Fairmont as clouds above us darken, unleashing a torrent of rain upon our arrival.

Gearhart gets out, goes in, and reappears, clothes drenched. "Not much charm, but we've run out of options. Here's a key. I'll be in the bar."

"What about this dog?"

Gearhart either doesn't hear or doesn't want to hear.

12.

Gearhart isn't in Whiskey Joe's. And that doesn't surprise me when I see how drab and sparse it is. I think maybe I've begun by now to understand something about aesthetics, at least as Gearhart perceives them.

I find him on the other side of the catering zone, a patio with high-top tables, each with its own mini gas fire pit in the middle. He has a midget martini glass in front of him.

"Bombay Sapphire," he says. "Just a one-ounce pour, like that tavern in Cedar City. No problem, it just means I'll have two."

Beyond the patio is a large pool of thermal spring water and a monster slide.

"I've never seen a resort for the middle-class," says Gearhart. "That's what this is: a vacation getaway for whole families. A shoebox of a room, fluorescent light fixtures—I can't even see into my suitcase—and paper cups in the bathroom. But anything beats Butte."

Me? I think it's awesome, all these pretty young things in bikinis by the pool. "I could tap into some of that," I say.

And with my penchant for big behinds, I think the babes tending bar aren't so bad either.

Gearhart is more interested in the Mile High Dining Room menu.

"This place looks okay," he says. "I don't understand why everyone is eating over there." He points to the Springwater Café.

"Easy," I say. "Middle America likes burgers and fries and onion rings. Come to think of it, I wouldn't mind a burger and fries myself."

Gearhart shakes his head. "Go to it. You're not my prisoner."

Truth be known, I was starting to enjoy hanging with Gearhart—and even the kind of food he eats.

"What did you do with the dog?" says Gearhart.

"Snuck him into my room. No name tag, nothing. Not even a collar."

"Probably a stray Bart picked up."

"You think he left him in the car on purpose?"

"Maybe. Doesn't matter, either way," says Gearhart. "All that matters is what we do with him. Finding Bart is not an option."

"What do you suggest?"

"The pound?"

"He wouldn't last a week in one of those places!"
I say.

"What's *your* option?"

"I don't know."

"You're not thinking of keeping him? You can barely look after yourself."

"Thanks a lot."

"Sleep on it. Problems are best assessed with fresh eyes."

"Where we headed tomorrow, boss?"

"I had it in my mind to head east, maybe Devil's Tower, then Colorado, the Rockies. But we've already turned west and I hate to backtrack."

"Okay . . ."

"Boise, Idaho. Never been there. After *this* . . ."—he gestures around—". . . I'll be ready for a city fix."

"Boise? How do you know it won't be like Butte?"

Gearhart shrugs. "I don't. And if it is, we'll keep moving."

At least Boise is south, so we're probably at the farthest point we'd get.

After a second mini martini, Gearhart shifts to the Mile High Dining Room and orders us the chef's special, Huckleberry Buffalo: grilled buffalo tenders, pickled cauliflower, garlic and horseradish mashed potato, and grilled asparagus, and a bottle of Elk Cove pinot noir from Willamette Valley, Oregon.

I've *never* before experienced a chef stopping by to ask my opinion about his cooking. But here he is, Chef Joshua, from Wyoming, standing over me.

"How's everything tasting?" he asks.

My mouth is too full to answer so I just nod, and try to hide the grilled buffalo I've stuffed in a linen serviette for the rogue dog in my room.

Gearhart says all the right things, and we finish up sharing a hot chocolate brownie à la mode before he says, "I've had enough for one day," and he gets up to go. He must be reading my mind, because he looks me in the eye and says, "Don't stay up too late—you need to be fresh tomorrow," and he's gone before I can ask him how old he thinks I am.

Of course, I'm not done, not with Whiskey Joe's nearby, a piano player named Danny Roy, and a bar server from Butte named Monique—maybe I'll get lucky.

13.

After we close the bar, Monique wants to show me her favorite dive, so I follow her back to Butte, somewhere near the historic district Gearhart and I circled hours earlier.

I drink a beer, then another, and maybe a shot of Fireball, because that's what everyone else in Pissers Palace is drinking, like everywhere else in the country, God knows why. And don't you know, right under my nose Monique hooks up with her ex-boyfriend—using me to get him re-interested. It results in a scuffle, initiated by the ex to prove his worthiness, I guess.

I bolt and, not five minutes after pulling onto the barren interstate, I have bacon on my tail.

Easy does it. Slow down. But not fast enough.

The cruiser's lights flash bright; I pull to a stop on the shoulder.

An officer of the Montana Highway Patrol gets out, a flashlight in one hand, the other on the butt of his holstered revolver.

I lower my window only partway.

He nods at me, flashes his light around Abe's interior. "Please turn off your engine."

I kill it.

"Where are you coming from?" he asks.

"California."

"I mean this evening."

"Butte." Talking to a cop is the same as giving a deposition: use as few words as possible. They only get used against you.

"Where in Butte?"

"I don't know Butte."

"Have you had any alcoholic beverages this evening?"

"Don't you need *reasonable cause* to pull me over, officer?"

"Speeding is reasonable. How many drinks have you had this evening?"

"Just one beer, officer."

"License and registration. And your engine key."

"My key?"

"Yes."

I fumble around my wallet, glove compartment, hand them over.

He returns to his cruiser, does his checks, comes back. "Please step out of your vehicle."

Standing before me, he flashes his light into my eyes. "Follow my finger from left to right and back again."

I do.

"Okay, now I want you to take nine steps straight ahead, pivot around, and take nine steps back toward me."

I do this, reasonably well, I think.

"I'm going to ask you take a breath test," he says.

"Aww, come on. Maybe I had two beers, but it was over a few hours. I'm in control."

"In Montana, if you refuse to take a breath test we take away your license for six months."

I shake my head. "So let's get it over with."

He holds his gizmo to my mouth. "Blow hard into this."

I do. Gently. Alcohol sits at the bottom of the lungs.

"Blow harder!"

I pretend to blow with greater force.

"Harder!"

I disengage. "I'm blowing as hard as I can."

He consults his digital readout. "You're under arrest for driving under the influence." And then he reads me my rights.

As if to reinforce his point, reinforcement turns up: another cruiser with another patrolman.

They cuff me, dump me in the backseat of the first cruiser; back to Butte we go.

The officer politely tries to engage me in conversation, as if he's my buddy, about where I'd been drinking—more evidence—but I gently assert my right to remain silent.

The large round clock in the police station says 1:03 as I get checked in.

"I'm thirsty," I say.

"Haven't had enough to drink?" quips the check-in sergeant.

"Water."

He points to a drinking fountain.

My hands are still cuffed but I go for broke. Dilution. Until the arresting officer depresses the button while I'm still leaning in, hydrating myself.

"Wouldn't want you messing up my blood test results," he says.

Must be a quiet night in Butte. I'm it.

Half an hour later, the vampire shows up. He seems hip, just cutting a life in this sad town. He finds a vein, sucks my blood.

After that, the sergeant says, "You can sleep it off here or get someone to pick you up."

"What about Abe?"

"Who's Abe?"

"My car."

"Impounded. You can collect it when you're sober."

"Okay, I'll call someone."

"We do that for you. Name and number?"

I give him Gearhart's name. "I don't have a number. He's at the Fairmont Resort."

I'm waiting about three hours—or so it seems—until the sergeant finally reappears and wordlessly unlocks my cage, leads me out.

Gearhart is standing there, rumpled and weary, shaking his mane.

"You're free to go," says the sergeant.

Gearhart leads me out to a waiting taxi.

"What took you?" I say.

Gearhart smirks. "I suppose I could have gotten here an hour earlier."

We ride mostly in silence back to the Fairmont.

As we're pulling into the resort, Gearhart says, "Nothing good can happen between midnight and six in the morning." And then he adds, "Now that you've got a dog, you've got to be more responsible."

14.

I'm up early. Coffee. Water. Food. And I wangle the Fairmont to ride me on a shuttle into Butte, the police pound. I barely have enough cash to cover the towing fee, but I pay up and skedaddle back to the resort—and Gearhart, waiting in the lobby.

"Boise?" I say.

"Boise," Gearhart confirms. "The cops do that?"

"Do what?"

"Your black eye."

"Huh?" I hadn't noticed. "No." I shake my head. "Happened at a bar."

Gearhart smirks. "Over a girl," he mumbles. "It's always over a girl. I hope you gave him one back."

"Wasn't worth it."

"Always stand up to a bully. Whatever you get, give it back twice as hard."

"I believe you, but right now I recommend a snappy departure."

"Why? You have someone *else* after you?"

"No," I whisper. "Pablo redecorated my room. I think he got inspired by Chef Joshua's Huckleberry Buffalo."

Gearhart places his right hand over his eyes, a *see no evil* moment.

I grab my things and snuggle Pablo—my Chihuahua—beneath my shirt, settle him on some dirty clothes in the backseat, and we hit the road. On this day there is little else before us (few other cars, this way or that) and some of the most astonishing scenery I've ever seen, and an appreciation of what people mean by the words *big sky*: left, right, front, and back, the sky is huge, with clouds sitting on far-off horizons.

By late morning my stomach is groaning.

"Any chance *I* can decide where to stop for something to eat?"

"Wouldn't that be like rewarding your bad behavior?"

"Hey, I didn't choose bad with that root beer place, Frostop."

"What would be today's choice?"

I make my case for Subway, the sandwich chain, and make myself even hungrier talking about it.

"On one condition," says Gearhart. "Your treat."

"Agreed."

"You ever attend college?"

"Sure I did—a BA in History from UCSB. Then I discovered there's not much I could do with it."

"You could get a master's and teach."

"Teaching may be the worst profession of my time. I take the occasional computer science course at City College."

"What will you *do* with it?"

"I'm going to create an app, make millions of dollars so I can surf every day and eat *indigenous* like you every night."

"That's like buying a lottery ticket," says Gearhart. "For every success story there are a million failures. Not that you shouldn't try, but don't dwell on it."

"But you said yourself, reality is money."

"It is. You need it. Find a niche for yourself in the computer world, if that's your passion."

"My passion is surfing."

"Can you teach it?"

"Can't stand having kooks around me."

"Kooks?"

"Beginners. They seriously get in the way, you know?"

"You know?"

"What kind of niche are you talking about?"

"A gap that people need but no one is paying attention to."

"Look." I point to a sign ahead. "Idaho Falls, Subway, Exit 118."

I pull in, park, and beeline for teriyaki chicken on cheese jalapeno bread with everything on it. Gearhart opts for turkey, jack cheese, lettuce, tomato, avocado, and olive oil. And I buy a roast beef sandwich for Pablo, hold the bread and trimmings.

After gnawing through half the sandwich, I ask, "So what's your idea of a gap or a niche in the computer world?"

"Off the top of my head?" Gearhart gingerly picks up his sandwich, bites into it, and chews. "The Internet is almost everyone's biggest source of information these days. Not necessarily the best, but the biggest."

"That's a no-brainer."

"And where does everyone go for fundamental reference-type information?"

"Google?"

"Beyond that, after they've done their Google search?"

"Where?"

"The free encyclopedia," says Gearhart.

"Wikipedia?"

"As far as I can tell, your generation, and especially the generation coming after yours, seems to think Wikipedia is the definitive word on any subject. Yet it is a free-for-all on which anyone may contribute, so long as they follow a particular writing style and cite their information with references."

"Your point?" I manage this through a major chomp-and-chew.

"Anything can be cited, even if it's with bogus Internet posts. Wikipedia has been compromised. And will continue to be corrupted, because there is no real control behind it, just a network of volunteers, each of whom has no more control than anyone else who is willing to learn Wikipedia-speak and wants to write or edit."

"Like I said, your point?"

"Let's say *you* become a whiz at Wikipedia," says Gearhart. "You can hire yourself to clients who want the truth told in a way they want readers to believe it."

"That's totally twisted, dude."

"Exactly. Everyone twists the truth. They put their own spin on what they want people to know about them. Whether it's politics or advertising or propaganda. Since everyone under forty years old puts their trust in Wikipedia, you can control, on behalf of a paying client, what they think of as the truth."

"Is that what the government does?"

"That's what *some* foreign governments are doing. I'm not sure ours is smart enough to have figured it out yet. They're too busy sucking up data from everywhere that they'll never have time to assess for lack of human resources."

"Who would pay?"

"People or companies concerned about their image. It's about subtle tweaks."

"Is there a course I can take on Wikipedia?"

Gearhart shrugs. "Who knows? Could be. I'm just using it as an example."

Back in the car, I hand-feed Pablo, a little at a time.

"You're spoiling him with roast beef," says Gearhart. "And he's going to need a walk for recycling."

"What I need is a pet store."

"Boise," says Gearhart.

"I may also need some cash."

"For what?"

"Dog stuff: a leash, a collar, a dish, dog food."

"Your dog, your tab," says Gearhart.

"Wait a second, Bart was *your* idea."

"I already told you my solution: a pound."

"How can you let this dog die? That's what they'll do, you know."

"It's not our problem."

"Sure it is. Pablo has been put in our laps."

"Once you get beyond the idea of the pound, he's in your lap, not mine."

"That's not fair."

"Unfairness is the history of the world."

"Can I at least *borrow* the money?"

"Against what?"

"You need collateral?"

"I need something."

"I don't *have* anything."

"All right," says Gearhart. "I guess I can loan you a hundred bucks on faith."

Down the interstate we come upon a road sign for a town called Bliss.

"Let's see what Bliss looks like," says Gearhart.

I ramp off. The town is just a beaten-up road-house opposite a used tractor lot. And then we can't ramp back on because of road maintenance and must double back ten miles just to rejoin the interstate.

"You know what the lesson is here?" says Gearhart.

"No, what?"

"Never trust Bliss. Or, as James Joyce wrote: 'In times of happiness, don't despair; misery is just around the corner.'"

Somewhere down the road, to our left, we see a traveling fair with a Ferris wheel and other amusements.

Gearhart sniffs the air in that way of his, when he seems satisfied with something, points it out as we pass by. "Always gives me a good feeling."

"Not me."

"You don't like funfairs?"

"No."

"Why not?"

"Whenever I went to one as a kid I always saw other kids having a great time with their dads."

Gearhart dips into his bag, plucks something out, and pushes it on me. "Put this in the CD player."

I oblige him and, for my sins, must endure not only *The Best of Dion and the Belmonts*, but also Gearhart's whistling.

"You know what the rule of whistling is, don't you?" I finally say.

"No."

"If you're not adding to the soundscape, it must go."

"You obviously don't know what the central rule of the road is, do you?"

"What is it?"

"Whoever pays for gas, makes the rules."

We pull into Boise early, around three o'clock, and after pulling into The Grove Hotel—tall and modern—I discover my toothpaste has leaked onto everything in my plastic J. C. Penney bag, and also made its way around Abe's interior.

"How'd that happen?" asks Gearhart, mildly amused.

"I lost the cap in my hotel bathroom."

Gearhart sighs. "I guess the lesson here is, if you can't cap it, lose it."

He gets out and checks us in.

"No pets," he says, handing me a key.

"Pablo can stay in Abe. He already staked it out anyway . . ."

"I know." Gearhart pinches his nose, turns to leave.

"Hold on," I say, "I know you're going out to scout everything, like you did in Jackson."

He nods.

"Do you mind if I tag along, see how you figure out where to eat and whatever else?"

Gearhart smiles. "See you down here in fifteen minutes."

15.

The first thing Gearhart does is ask the concierge for one of their local maps, and the second is ask their recommendations for drinks and dinner. (When he's done, I find out about the nearest, cheapest pet store.)

Then he sets out, this time with me in tow.

"I understand they have a revitalized historic downtown," he says, as we stride Grove Street. "But I'm not holding my breath."

"That's cynical."

He winks. "The key to happiness is low expectations."

Ninth Street brings a smile to his eyes. "This is what I had hoped of Butte, of anywhere. A revitalized historical district." He looks around in amazement "Boise. Who would've known?"

From beat-up Butte to buoyant Boise.

"What is it you're seeing?" I ask.

"It's clean, well maintained. Even the modern architecture is tasteful, side by side with preserved historic structures. And everyone is so polite, friendly. That's the America I remember."

We turn left. Gearhart scopes out a wine bar called Bodovina, part of a galleria of shops and art studios, one containing the work of a nocturnal artist that exaggerates light as contrast against the dark. Gearhart notes the artist's name. ("For my daughter. She's always on the lookout for fresh approaches to nocturnes.")

Out he goes, across Ninth to the R. Grey Gallery, an artsy jeweler's. I follow him and watch as he pokes around, absorbing whatever he finds of interest. He zeroes in on a display case, a collection called REALSTEEL.

"What's the story on this?" he asks a female sales assistant. "I've never seen anything like it."

"My father's line," she replies. "Made from recycled steel and gems. He likes to think of his creations as sculpture you can wear."

I point to a pin: a twisted railroad nail with a red gemstone in the center. "That's cool."

"Why do you like it?" asks Gearhart.

"The symbolism. *Nailed.*"

"You think of yourself as a martyr?"

"It's been rough," I say. "I'm not complaining, but it speaks to me."

He nods, looks around some more, and then we're out, strolling Ninth again.

We pass Lucky Fins seafood restaurant, which the concierge mentioned.

"Reminds me of Subway," says Gearhart. "One notch above fast food."

Further on: a Ruth's Chris Steakhouse.

"Good to know," says Gearhart. "But I try to avoid chains, even the quality ones."

One more block, and Gearhart nails it: a bar and tapas-style restaurant called Juniper.

"Here's where I will be at 6:33," he says, his recon at an end. "Now I'm going back to my room for a nap."

And I head to Petco for supplies.

16.

An admission here: I have a pet peeve of almost pathological proportions.

I hate when people talk loudly, or at all, on cell phones in public places, like in bars and restaurants.

When they do this—and it happens a lot—I am compelled to glare at the perpetrator and, if they don't get the message, I speak loud enough to whomever I'm with, or to myself if I'm alone, so the gabber can hear how rude I think he or she is.

When they ignore me, as they always do, I speak louder and louder, until it causes them to either terminate their call or nervously go outside and finish it. Sometimes they complain, and once in a while it gets me booted from whatever bar or restaurant I'm in.

My beach buddies get a kick out of it, maybe not realizing how serious I am, or how unable I am to control it.

Anyway, Gearhart is not amused when I start sounding off in Juniper about a rude bitch down the bar having a drawn out conversation with someone and sharing details of her life nobody around us wants to know.

"People with cell phones need to learn some manners," I say, loud enough for everyone to hear.

Gearhart is drinking a Junipero gin martini next to me at the bar. "I'm trying to enjoy my cocktail," he says. "Knock it off."

"How can we enjoy a drink," I say loudly, "when that obnoxiously rude bitch spouts off about her personal life for all to hear? As if anyone cares."

"You're the one acting obnoxious."

"It's not an act, man. I really mean it."

"Keep it up and either you're leaving or *I'm* leaving."

Another minute passes and this bitch is still yakking away like there's no tomorrow, and I erupt: "I just can't believe how friggin' rude some people are with their cell phones! This is noise pollution!"

Gearhart gets off his stool, grabs his martini glass, cocktail napkin, and shaker, and moves clear down to the other side of the bar.

So I figure, what the hell, he's an old fart and I'm doing *him* a favor hanging out when I could be chasing tail. The night awaits me.

Another admission: I have a bit of an authority problem. I'm just real sensitive about getting told off.

So, I think, *he wants me to go away?*

I'm gone, man. *Adios amigo* (as much as it grieves me to walk out on the buffalo meatballs we ordered).

I walk briskly to the hotel with my dark thoughts, wondering why I'd stuck around this long with a crotchety old sourpuss. Like, *he's* such great company?

I throw everything into my J. C. Penney bags, go down, and climb into Abe with Pablo, who in my absence laid a couple of small turds on the front passenger seat.

I clean up the mess (fortunately, I bought paper towels and sanitary spray at Petco), lower all the windows, give it a moment, and burn rubber, leaving Boise in my rearview mirror, where it belongs.

I get on I-84 West and cut south on Route 95, straddling the border with Oregon for another twenty minutes before my temper subsides and I start to reason it through.

I *am* irrational about rude cell phone users, damn them.

Gearhart *did* give me a warning, which I did not heed.

In a strange sort of way, I kind of missed the old buzzard. This would not be the right way to end our road trip.

I look at Pablo, who's sitting in the front passenger seat—Gearhart's seat—and he looks mournful, like he too misses Gearhart.

"You don't really want to go back and get him, do you?"

Pablo winks at me—a good one-eye wink.

"What? All right. But if it weren't for *me* you'd be on death row right now."

So I turn around and follow my tracks all the way back to the Grove, decide that Gearhart must be in for the night, none the wiser about my abrupt departure, and rejoin the buzz on Ninth Street after tucking Pablo into his backseat bed.

By this time, mid-evening, it is alive with young people—bohemians, hipsters, and colorful characters—and some of the most gorgeous gals I've ever seen, dressed in skirts and dresses and made up for the night much nicer than the faux blonde and Botox brigade in southern Cal.

I do a couple of dive bars in the Basque neighborhood—Pengilly's Saloon, Whiskey Bar, a couple shots, hand out dollar bills to a war vet and a mother of three (says their signs)—and straggle back to the Grove. On impulse, I keep walking; a nightcap, maybe, and I find myself standing outside Bodovino, that wine bar Gearhart scouted upon arrival.

I go in, and there he is, Gearhart, sitting at the bar, a glass of red wine in front of him.

I broadside him. "Late for you, isn't it?"

He smiles wide. "Much too late. Allow me to introduce you to Stephanie."

I look around and face an awesomely attractive young woman behind the bar. Long dark hair, peach complexion, big brown eyes, and shapely, oh so shapely.

"Stephanie just finished her master's in business at Boise State University," says Gearhart. "I've been telling her about you."

"*Me*?"

"How you live on the American Riviera and that you're on the verge of huge success in the dot-com world." He winks at me.

Clearly, she has eaten up every word, looking at me like I'm some kind of pop star.

"I've been wanting to visit Santa Barbara forever," she gushes. "Now I'll know somebody there."

We exchange contact details in our phones and she goes off to serve another customer after pouring me a taster of pinot noir.

"How did you spend the evening?" asks Gearhart, as if nothing had happened between us.

I guess I'm truly oversensitive; to him it hardly mattered.

"Uh, I took a long walk, a hike, really, up through the residential neighborhood behind the Capitol building."

"I walked around the Capitol as the sun was setting," says Gearhart. "Unbelievably accessible. Not one security officer in sight, no paranoia. Our leaders in Washington could learn a thing or two from this place. I'd trade Boise for DC any day of the week."

I am surprised to see Gearhart somewhat tipsy. The odd word slurred, eyes a wee bit red and watery.

I open my billfold and pluck a five-ski. "You won."

"Won?"

"Bart. He knew something I didn't."

Gearhart waves it away.

"A bet is my word." I smack it on the bar next to him, and by the wry smile on his lips I think he appreciates a lesson taught, and learned.

Stephanie reappears. "How's that wine?"

"Great. I'll take a whole glass."

Gearhart picks up Honest Abe, studies it, smirking, as if it's maybe counterfeit. "This isn't currency. This is a *debit* note."

"What do you mean by that?"

"Our country is seventeen trillion dollars in debt, and rising. We're in hock. No wonder I see pawn-shops and consignment shops everywhere we go in Middle America. We no longer produce anything of any substance, no manufacturing, and no indus-try, all subcontracted to countries with slave labor. The only thing we export anymore is fast food." He drains his wine. "While I was overseas protecting my country, it got sold out from under me."

"That's heavy, dude."

"No. The heavy part is the burden that will crush the shoulders of newer generations of Americans."

This is a side I'd not seen of Gearhart till now; must be the sauce talking.

"Who are you really, dude?" I ask.

"Really, truly?" He grins.

"Uh-huh, I'd like to know."

"I knew your dad."

"WHAT?"

Gearhart pulls his whimsical shrug. "I'm sur-prised you haven't figured it out by now."

I cannot believe what I'm hearing. "Figured out what?"

"Your dad and I worked on a tour together over-seas. He's still there, as far as I know. When I last saw him—it was some time ago—he wanted me to check in on you, see how you're getting along in life. I promised I would."

I'm standing there dumbfounded, not knowing what to say, and then the twinkle in Gearhart's eye suddenly freezes and he grimaces in pain, grabs his gut.

"Are you okay?" I ask, still in a daze from his bombshell revelation.

"Yes, fine, probably a gallbladder attack, nothing serious. It'll subside. I guess I had too much fun tonight."

A long moment elapses and I feel, given the hour and his booze intake, it's okay to get personal.

"I'm sorry about your wife," I say. "How long were you married?"

"Thirty-three years." He looks down at the bar.

"That's a long time, dude, especially these days."

"Didn't feel like it." He looks up again, a bittersweet smile. "That's what happens when you stay in motion. We moved a lot. I think it makes life go faster."

"What was she like?"

Gearhart seems about to say something, stops himself, and starts again. "She had a great sense of humor. That's what kept us together in difficult times." His lips tighten, and his eyes, watery from drink, overflow into a tear. "Miss her every day." He gets up, embarrassed, and attempts to cover up with a quick elbow movement followed by a waist-high wave good night.

I climb off my stool and face him. "Mister Gearhart? Can you tell me more about my dad?"

He waves me off, but I offer a hug, arms outstretched, partly because I'm moved by what he just laid on me, and partly because I feel like a fool for almost running away earlier.

Gearhart accepts, even holds a beat longer than I'd intended. And then without further word he goes off into the night, leaving me in Bodovina to chitchat with the bodo-vacious Stephanie.

17.

Next morning.

I'm up early, down to see Pablo, who's already wagging his tail whenever he sees me. A quick walk to get his business done before conducting ours: the road.

"Where we headed, boss?"

"You decide."

"C'mon. You must have somewhere in mind."

"Not today."

"Let me see your map." I assess the options. "The most direct route back to Santa Barbara is through Nevada."

"I've decided I hate Nevada."

"So we'll go west through Oregon, drop through northern California."

"Bend," says Gearhart.

"Huh?"

"Bend, Oregon. I've heard it's pleasant. From what I've seen, I'm guessing there are only about three dozen places in the United States that are worthy of an overnight stay. The rest are like Butte and Cedar City."

"You couldn't kill a night in a normal place?"

"Life is too short."

"Just one night?"

"Not if you live your life as if every day is your last."

"Is that what you do?"

"The present is the most important gift you've got. The magic is in the moment. Look after the moment and the hours, days, and weeks will look after themselves."

"You seem more relaxed since we started," I say.

Gearhart nods. "I am."

The road to Bend from Idaho is all about, well, *bends*, around oddly shaped hills.

And speaking of *odd*, Pacific Time doesn't cut in until you're an hour into the Beaver State, almost as if a large slice of eastern Oregon is really Idaho, but you know it's Oregon because you're not allowed to pump your own gas—state law—and it's cleaner and greener than anywhere we've been.

"How's your gallbladder today?"

"Better."

"Does that happen a lot?"

"Depends how much fun I'm having."

And then I drop my bomb. "What you said about knowing my father . . . ?" I trail off.

"Is that what I said?" Gearhart shakes his head. "I had too much to drink last night, didn't know what I was talking about." He takes one of his deep breaths, doesn't even look at me.

"But . . ."

Gearhart shrugs, says nothing more, a body language that says finality.

We are both hungry, but most of the route is scenery and road, and the few small towns we encounter have little to offer. By noon, we figure we may as well wait until Bend for a bite.

Bite is exactly what's going on in Bend—their annual food festival. Central streets are closed off to cars and filled with stalls run by local restaurateurs offering small portions of their best dishes for a few bucks.

We come upon the Oxford Hotel. Its look pleases Gearhart, who has been otherwise not very talkative and maybe a little hungover. He saunters in, as usual, to scope it out.

"Most expensive hotel yet," he says, opening the back door to grab his satchel. "But what the hell, let's celebrate."

"Celebrate what?"

"Today is Father's Day."

"*Celebrate*?" I shake my head. "That was the worst friggin' day of the year for me growing up! What about *your* dad?"

"Long gone."

"How long?"

"He died when I was nine."

"How?"

"Some kind of gut cancer."

The Oxford's lobby is like a yoga studio, all lightness and space.

And the room . . . Damn, if I thought the Wort was nice, *this* replaces it as the best room I've ever had in my life. Even the bedding . . . just give me a sleeping bag and sofa bed and I'm good . . . but this? Something called Frette, says the brochure. A spoiler.

Next I discover this place has a complimentary Laundromat—and even the detergent is free! Timing couldn't be better since I'm wearing the last of my J. C. Penney threads and most of my clothes now smell like Pablo.

And then I discover—glancing at their brochure—that this place is pet friendly.

I call down. "You mean my dog can come in?"

"You usually have to reserve in advance," he says. "But we can do it. There is a fifty-five dollar charge, but that includes a pet bed and organic treats."

"I'm in."

Hell, Gearhart could add it to my tab.

"We can also offer you dog walking, grooming, and pet massage."

Pet massage?

"I'm in for a grooming and massage. What time can you fit him in?"

"Hold on, I'll check." Moments later. "We can do it right now."

I go down, collect Pablo, deliver him to the groomer, and launch to the food festival to feed: a slice of pizza here, Thai noodles further on, chicken curry beyond that.

I assume Gearhart is around somewhere—he needed to eat, too—but I don't want to search him out, intrude on his alone time. And, in fact, I neither see nor hear from him the rest of the afternoon as I do my laundry and take a long hot bath, for whatever reason assuming we'd do our own thing come evening, me and Pablo, fresh and clean with a blue ribbon affixed to his collar.

After the festival ends at six o'clock, the streets go quiet and Bend is deserted.

At 6:33 my room phone rings.

"I'm going to a place called the Pine Tavern for a cocktail and dinner," says Gearhart. "Feel welcome."

"Are you sure?"

"I dragged you along on this road trip, so I've got to make sure you're fed."

"No, really. Don't feel like you have to entertain me."

But he had already hung up.

18.

"Happy Father's Day," says Gearhart, raising his martini glass at the Pine Tavern's bar.

"I told you," I say. "It's not something I celebrate."

"You've got to get over it."

"Why?"

"So you can move on. It seems to be holding you back from getting on with your life. How do you think *I* felt when I lost my father at nine years old?"

"At least you had one."

"Granted. And he got stolen from me just when I started to need him most. So I *knew* what I was missing. It took a long time—a real long time—and you never really get over it, but you get *on* with it."

"How?"

"Buy yourself a lockbox, a little safe with a key. Then grab a pen and paper and write down everything you feel about Father's Day, about amusement parks, about not knowing your dad. Write it all down—everything—no matter how long it takes or how much paper you need. And when you're done, place it in the box and lock it away. That's where it shall remain thereafter. Once a year, if you feel like it, maybe on Father's Day, you can open the box and revisit what you wrote. And then put it back and lock it up again."

"Why do you think he didn't want to know me?"

"How do you know he didn't?"

"People have choices."

"Life gets complicated. Or so it seems to people until the passage of time offers perspective."

"But in Boise you said you knew him."

"Did I say that? On the day of my father's funeral," continues Gearhart, "my mother gave me his wristwatch. I've worn it every day since. Nothing special, just an old Benrus. But it gave me comfort."

"I don't have anything."

"I'm sorry."

"For what?"

"For taking up your time like this without advance notice," says Gearhart, digging into wild Chinook salmon.

"Nah, it's been good to get away." I look down. "I didn't want to take this job, tried my best to get out of it. But now I'm not sure I want to return." I look back up again, shake off the sentiment. "These hotels are just *too* good. Where are you going after this?"

"I don't know," Gearhart says quietly.

"What do you mean?"

"Just what I said. I don't know. That's the truth. Why are you asking?"

"I don't know, maybe to stay in touch? I've never learned so much in a few days as I have traveling with you, you know."

"You know."

"Well?"

"We'll see. This road trip isn't over yet."

19.

Next morning: early to rise after early to bed, and a spectacular view of a rising sun on Mts. Faith, Hope, and Charity—and Mount Bachelor farther to the east. I had checked out the Astro Lounge, recommended by Bronwyn, our server at the Pine Tavern, but after popping my head in, I just didn't feel like staying out late drinking.

In the lobby I encounter Gearhart scowling at his bill. "Thirty bucks for a dog massage?"

"Pablo was stressed," I say. "Traveling is tough on him. Deduct it from my tip."

"What makes you think you deserve one after getting me out of bed at two thirty in the morning to haul you out of the clink?"

"C'mon—look at him."

Pablo is still sporting his blue ribbon.

Gearhart shakes his head, attempting dismay, veiling a grin.

The trunk roads are lined with pine trees that soon give way to redwoods, among the tallest and oldest in the world: whole long stretches—pure and green with towering sequoias on either side. In just a few days, after I started paying attention, I've seen a good amount of Mother Nature.

"Looks like we'll drive through Grant's Pass," says Gearhart, studying his map. "There's someone I'd like to look up near there, in Jacksonville."

"Your call, boss."

I hadn't seen him use a cell phone before, but crafty old Gearhart pulls one out of his bag—nothing fancy, just a flip phone—and he plays with it a bit, fitting the battery, I think. He gingerly taps out a number and has a mumbled conversation with someone.

"Okay," he says to me when he's done. "Instead of going west when we reach I-5, we need to go east, get off at Medford."

We find the house belonging to Gearhart's friend at the very top of a dead-end road on a hill.

"Wait here," says Gearhart.

He gets out and rings the doorbell, and waits. And waits. And waits.

Finally, an old man answers, scraggly gray hair and liver spots all over his face. He must have been ninety years old.

They hug, exchange a few words, and Gearhart walks over to where I'm waiting inside Abe with my window down.

"I thought we'd take my old friend out for lunch, but I can see it's not easy for him to go anywhere. So I'm just going to sit and visit with him for a few minutes."

"Go for it." I alight, open the passenger door, let Pablo out to pay his dues.

It takes Gearhart's friend a good five minutes, one small step at a time, to get from his front door to a bench on the front patio.

Gearhart sits with him, and they chat.

His friend fumbles with a canvas bag, pulls out an oxygen tank, and attaches it to his nose.

They seem to be reminiscing. I catch only snippets of hushed chatter. Paris, Beirut, Baghdad. This name, that name.

Finally, Gearhart helps him up and back to his front door, sees him in, returns to the car.

"Poor old bastard," he says. "I didn't know he has COPD."

"What's that?"

"Lung disease. He smoked like a fiend. Getting old is tough. His mind is as sharp as a tack. I think I'd prefer it the other way around: a working body and dementia, a mental fade-out instead of physical breakdown. In fact, I'd rather not be seventy-nine."

"That's not old."

"It is for him."

"I could tell."

"I think I'm the only one from the old shop who's ever been to his house." He pauses. "Friends are important. Do you have any?"

"Any? You think I have no friends?"

"True friends are rare," says Gearhart. "I could have asked if you have *many* friends, but fewer is truer. You only need less than a handful."

"Need for what?"

"To talk to, share experiences, reference points for more talking."

"I guess I have one or two like that."

"Do they go back a long way?"

I shrug. "I'm not good at staying in touch."

"Are they a positive influence on your life?"

"Why is that important?"

"People partly become who they associate with."

"Oh, like peer pressure?"

"No, beyond that. Grown-up friends."

"You're assuming I've grown up."

Gearhart nods, says something under his breath like, *finally, it's taken long enough.*

I let it pass.

"Who's your *best* friend?" he asks.

I consider this, deeply. "My mother," I finally say.

Gearhart smiles.

"You think that makes me a momma's boy?"

"No. I think it's charming. Does she know where you are?"

"She knows I'm driving someone on a road trip."

"Most people make friends where they work," says Gearhart. "That's not the best way. You can lose them, based on how things play out in the work-place."

"Never been a problem for me!"

Gearhart chuckles, gets it.

"I gather it's been a problem for you," I add.

He nods. "When I reached a senior position, it became my job to decide who got promoted and who went where. My friends had high expectations, but my decisions were based on merit, so I lost a few. That guy I just saw . . ." Gearhart shakes his head. "One of the best. Such a shame." He pauses. "Let me tell you something: If, when you awaken in the morning, you do not have to deal with doctors or lawyers or tax collectors, and you can walk without assistance to dinner, and then, for one night anyway, you can afford to eat and drink anything you want, you're doing damn good."

20.

Officialdom welcomes us at Oregon's border with California.

Gearhart is incredulous. "A customs post?"

I ease Abe to a halt.

"Where you coming from?" asks a uniformed officer.

"Oregon, Montana, Wyoming, Idaho, Utah . . ."

"Did you buy any fireworks?" asks a female officer.

"Nope," I say. "No fireworks."

"Okay. Go on ahead."

Gearhart shakes his head. "Glad to see they're finally cracking down on fireworks. Here." He jabs me with a CD.

"Not more Belmonts."

"No."

I pop it in and a melody emerges.

"You kidding me? Doris Day?"

Entering Humboldt County—the marijuana-growing capital of he world—I should be in my element. I'd been invited to Humboldt many times to help with the harvest. Ten grand for two weeks' work—and all you can smoke.

So I finally make it here and it's the first time in over twenty years I've gone five days straight without smoking. And I'm thinking, I'm doing just fine, maybe I'll keep going, see how long I can get by without it.

We hit the Pacific, a rocky and lush coastline. I pull onto a scenic rest stop so Gearhart can stretch his legs, take the view (and I can yank Doris Day).

"If you touch her," he says, reading my mind, "I'll start it over from the beginning."

At Eureka, Humboldt's largest city, I pull off the interstate to check out this beach town as a possible overnight.

"This haze ain't no fog," I say to Gearhart, mindful of Eureka's main industry.

Gearhart glances this way and that, unimpressed. "No epiphany here," he finally says. "Very scuzzy. Keep moving."

From the backseat, Pablo whines.

"I think Pablo wants to stay," I say.

"Pablo is more than welcome to remain."

"Okay, maybe he just wants a quick walk."

Waterfront Drive leads to a slice of sandy beach facing Eureka Channel.

I pull over and park behind a decrepit camper. From it, a hose runs across the sand.

Gearhart points it out. "I don't believe it," he says, shaking his head. "Those folks are emptying their septic tank in broad daylight. That's got to be illegal. Can you believe this town?"

I get out, open the back door for Pablo, and we scramble onto the sand.

Not three minutes later, a pit bull jumps out of the camper and barrels straight at us.

Pablo startles and yaps. I manage to scoop him up a split second before the pit bull would've snapped its jaws around little Pablo's neck. And still the muscular beast doesn't give up, standing on its hind legs, snarling and slobbering as I snuggle Pablo close to my chest.

The nearest thing I can lay my free hand on is an empty Bud Lite bottle somebody discarded on a low wall. I wave it at the pit bull to shoo it away.

Out of the corner of my eye I catch an unkempt dude in swim trunks bounding out of the camper. He's muscular, like his pit bull, but with a large paunch and multiple tattoos. I assume he's going to call his dog off, but instead he starts hollering, "Leave my fucking dog alone or I'm going to pound your ass!" He is buzzed; probably drank the beer from the bottle I'm holding.

"Your dog should be on a leash!" I holler back.

Gnarly Dude comes closer, laughing. "He's hungry, can't you see? He likes to snack on Chihuahuas before dinner. I think I'll feed him yours."

I glance thirty yards to where Gearhart is sitting inside the car, watching us.

Gnarly Dude hoots with derision as his pit bull continues to lunge with snapping jaws at Pablo, who's trembling, twisting, scared out of his wits, practically jumping out of my arms to get away.

I don't know what kind of power swell comes over me, but I swing the bottle sideways and whop it as hard as I can against the side of Gnarly Dude's head.

He goes down with a thud.

Next I toss the bottle at his pit bull, catching it smack in the face, and it scuttles back into the camper.

I tread sand back to Abe, jump in, and zip off.

Gearhart doesn't say a word. Until a minute or so later when he suggests we drive twenty miles south to Ferndale, the kind of Victorian town travel guides suggest as the right place to overnight in Humboldt County.

But we hardly arrive and Gearhart is shaking his head again, and keeps shaking it up and down Main Street. "I'm not staying here."

"What's wrong with it?"

"Forlorn," he replies. "Creepy."

"But it's already four thirty."

"Just get back on 101, keep going south. I know where we can overnight."

Garberville doesn't make the cut; neither does the Benbow Historic Inn, and we leave those places, also, in our wake.

"I hope I didn't hurt that guy," I finally say about my Humboldt Beach incident.

"He got what he deserved," growls Gearhart. "You protected your own and stood your ground. I'm proud of you."

21.

It is way past six thirty when we pull into Healdsburg, another marathon driving day.

"Turn left and pull in over there."

Gearhart guides me into the forecourt of Hotel
Healdsburg and climbs out.

By now, I know the drill.

"It's a stretch, price-wise," he says, returning.
"But what the hell? This is our last night."

"Really?"

I no longer want this road trip to end.

Our rooms aren't ready, so the management sends
us to the bar for complimentary cocktails while we
wait.

Gearhart is delighted to see his favorite gin, 209.

"Hello, Mister Gearhart," says the middle-aged
bartender, a long-term professional from the look
of him.

"You've been here before?" I say.

"Yes."

I look at him for further explanation, but he gives none.

Even after our receptionist delivers keys, Gearhart doesn't want to move; this is his longest martini yet.

"You can go ahead," he waves me on. "I've got a table booked in Dry Creek Kitchen, their restaurant next door."

Upstairs, by a long shot, *the* finest room of all: dark hardwood floors and teak furnishings; plantation shutters on French doors to a balcony overlooking Healdsburg's main square with a gazebo and a flagpole and everything I ever imagined a real hometown to be.

After showering and changing into freshly cleaned clothes, I descend to the restaurant and find Gearhart on their patio in the open air, with a bottle of red wine and a decanter.

"Opus One," he says. "You only live once."

I sit down, sip from my glass, utterly astonished. "I've never known anything like it."

"You look a lot different than the first morning I met you," says Gearhart. "You were wearing a tank top under a denim shirt. Now look at you."

In truth, I feel different, too: whether the clothes, the wine—or maybe the company.

Gearhart takes one of his deep nose breaths, relaxed, satisfied. "Do you have any religious beliefs?"

I shake my head. "I told you, I was brought up in a commune that believed in peace and love until it became inconvenient. My grandparents in Solvang wanted me to attend a Lutheran church with them, but I wasn't interested."

"What about spiritual beliefs as you grew up learning about the world for yourself?"

I pull a pendant from my shirt. "Saint Christopher. Patron saint of surfers. Why do you ask? Do you believe in God?"

"You'd have to define what you mean by God."

"God. You know, *God*."

"You know. It means many things to many cultures. Which god are you talking about?"

I pluck a one-dollar bill from my wallet, about all I have left. "See? *In God we trust*. That God."

Gearhart chuckles. "It's missing the *L*. I'd rather have it backed by gold than God."

"Then why are you asking me about God?"

"Just curious. I've been to places where no god exists, and based on what I've seen, I'm not even sure humankind deserves protection from a god. So you wonder, if there's no god, what is there?"

"The devil?"

"More believable."

"But how can you have one without the other?"

"I don't have the answer, just positing the question. I have another: Who was your idol as a child?"

I consider this for a few seconds. "My dad."

He absorbs this with surprise. "But you told me you never had one."

"I must have had a dad, or I wouldn't be here. So he was out there, somewhere, doing something." I pause, not wanting to get emotional about this, but my voice breaks anyway and my eyes well up. "And I always imagined it was something great, something heroic."

Gearhart swirls the wine in his glass, tight-mouthed, and suddenly reaches for his gut. "I must be having too much fun again. I think I'm about to have another gallbladder attack."

"Shouldn't you see someone about that?"

"Usually it subsides. If it gets worse, I go to the hospital for a shot of Demerol."

I consult the menu. "What's indigenous to Healdsburg?"

"We're in Sonoma County, where wine and food are celebrated beyond all else, and worshipped like God. You can order anything and it'll be the best."

"Can I have a hamburger?"

"You can have whatever you want."

In this place, a hamburger means *Wagyu Mini Burgers on Toasted Brioche with Black Truffle Aioli.* (I would never look at Tinker's mini-burgers the same way again.)

"I probably shouldn't ask for ketchup," I say to Gearhart.

"Probably not."

Dusk turns to dark, it's cooler, and a gas heater is switched on for us. Gearhart shows no sign of wanting to get up. He orders us both something called Armagnac, which he describes as "triple-refined cognac."

"It's not going to make your gallbladder worse?" I say.

He shrugs. "Sometimes it helps."

When finally he finishes, and Healdsburg is quiet, no diners left, no one on the streets, he gets up and crosses into the main square.

I check on Pablo, feed him some of the fancy burger meat I'd set aside, and scoop him up for a walk.

Gearhart, strolling way ahead, finally settles near the flagpole. He looks straight up at the fluttering stars and stripes in what I can only describe as a mournful gaze. In my mind I hear "Taps" playing.

I quietly leave Gearhart to his thoughts.

Tiptoeing away, toward the hotel, I hear Gear-hart ask after me, "Are you kind?"

I turn. "What?"

But he is already gone, somewhere in the shadows.

22.

I am where I'm supposed to be at 9:03 the next morning, as stipulated, for the hotel's complimentary breakfast.

Gearhart isn't.

The night before he seemed tired, worn out, so I assume he's sleeping late, or just taking his time, and I see it as an opportunity to engage in a *pre*-breakfast of cooked-to-order scramble with everything in it, set me up for waffles when he appears.

After waffles (I couldn't help myself), and no Gearhart, I hit up reception for his room number and use the house phone to call up to him, find out when he wants to hit the road (maybe he rose early, ate breakfast without me).

"Charles Gearhart?" she says. "He was taken to Healdsburg District Hospital late last night."

"Why?"

She shrugs, but I already have it figured out: the gallbladder attack got worse, he went in for a shot of Demerol, and they probably kept him for observation. Or maybe they took the damn thing out, which would mean he wasn't going anywhere today, or tomorrow.

"Where's the hospital?"

"About a mile away."

Her directions are simple.

I climb into Abe and, with Pablo at my side, find my way to University Avenue and stroll into the lobby, approach reception.

"Where can I find Charles Gearhart? He came in last night."

She consults a board, clacks her computer keyboard, and picks up her phone, exchanges a few words.

"He's coming down to see you," she says.

I'm waiting, and I realize I owe my mother a call from yesterday, so I phone her, tell her I'm fine, that I'm finally on my way home, hope to be back tonight, just waiting for news on my passenger, who had to go the hospital.

And—who the hell knows why—she finally asks my passenger's name.

"Gearhart," I say. "Charles Gearhart."

Silence.

"Mom, you there?"

"Yes." Silence. "Luke . . . ?"

I lose her to more silence or a patchy connection. Just when the line clears and she starts to speak, a man wearing scrubs and a stethoscope around his neck appears in front of me.

"Gotta go, Mom—I'll call you back." I turn to face him.

"I'm Doctor Bloomfield. You are?"

"Luke Andersen."

He nods solemnly.

I look over his shoulder. "I'm looking for Charles Gearhart."

"I know." He pauses. "I'm sorry to tell you, he expired."

"What?" I cannot believe my ears. "From a gallbladder attack?"

Dr. Bloomfield shakes his head. "No. He had pancreatic cancer."

"No, that's not . . . What the . . . ?" Now I'm feeling dizzy. I need to sit down. I stagger to a row of waiting-room chairs, nail one.

Dr. Bloomfield sits beside me, his hands on his knees. "I've been treating Charlie for six weeks."

"What are you talking about? *Who* are you talking about? Charlie *who*? Are we talking about the same person? How can you be treating him? He was just traveling through here—with me!"

"No. Charles Gearhart lived here, in Healdsburg. He found out just over six weeks ago that he was suffering from pancreatic cancer. The prognosis was terminal. He knew he had less than two months to live."

I'm sitting with my mouth agape, in a state of shock. "No, this can't be," I finally say. "We have a road trip to finish. Is this some kind of bad joke?" I look around frantically, willing Gearhart to appear.

"I'm sorry." He pauses. "Charlie told me there was something he needed to do. Then about a week ago he walked out on treatment—it wouldn't have helped anyway—and disappeared."

"When did this happen?"

"Your father passed at 5:33."

"No, no—you see, you got the wrong guy. He wasn't my father."

Dr. Bloomfield looks me square in the eye. "You're Luke Andersen, right?"

I nod my head, over and over again, uncontrollably, my eyes filling up so much that I can't even see straight. "Yes, I'm Luke Andersen, but . . ."

"If it's any comfort to you, your father was very happy at the end."

I can barely talk through trembling lips. "Happy? What do you mean, *happy*?"

"He told me that he finally got to know his son. That was very important to him."

I can no longer speak, my throat is so dry, and anyway, I don't have anything left to say.

"Your father told me all about you, Luke," says Dr. Bloomfield, holding out a large orange envelope. "He said he was very proud of how you had grown up. And he asked me to give you this."

I look down, not wanting to accept it, not wanting to accept anything.

"Please take it."

I numbly allow it to be placed in my lap.

"Are you okay, Luke?"

I shake my head, back and forth, back and forth. "No, I'm not okay." Tears are streaming down both my cheeks. "I'm definitely *not* okay."

"Would you like a prescription for a sedative?"

"No. No. I don't . . . I . . ."

Dr. Bloomfield stands and shakes my hand, tells me he's sorry again, that he's needed elsewhere, and disappears, and somehow I make it to my car, fuzzy and disoriented.

Sitting behind the wheel, I rip open the envelope he'd given me and its contents tumble into my lap. Gearhart's vintage wristwatch, the Benrus he wore that had belonged to his dad. A tiny pouch, which

I unbutton and find the railroad nail pin from that REALSTEEL jeweler in Boise, the one I told him I liked because of its symbolism. *Nailed.*

I can hardly believe he went back and bought it for me.

I feel something else in there, jostle the envelope, and out falls a small metal key with a plastic tag: AMERICAN RIVER BANK, 412 CENTER STREET, HEALDSBURG, CA, BOX 33.

And an un-smoked Macanudo and matches from a shop called Tobacco Row in Jackson, Wyoming.

23.

My mind is reeling as I pull Abe into a spot out-side Flying Goat Coffee and stagger with Pablo in my arms over to the Plaza, Healdsburg's main square, where I'd last seen Gearhart.

From motional to *emotional* blur. From sadness to anger, for not knowing sooner, say, while Gearhart was still alive, that he was my dad.

Why didn't he just tell me?

I'm dizzy, my mind trying to process too much, so I find a bench to sit on, beneath an oak tree, and try to regain my focus.

Anger passes, and the tears come and come, I'm crying my eyes out as if I were nine years old, and Pablo on my lap, trying to lick my face clean, drink my tears, soothe my hurt.

When I finally run out of tears, I just sit there, for a long, long time, thinking about Gearhart and our road trip together, my mind flashing back to different moments, things he said, until everything begins to crystalize into some kind of lit up chandelier.

When he called The Drive Cycle, he specifically requested me.

I vaguely recognized him because he had once or twice visited karaoke night at the bar, I guess to see me.

Our road trip began on my birthday.

He had lived for a short time in Monterey when my mother was in San Francisco nearby. That's when they must have met, because I got born around nine months later.

Took me to see Kemmerer, Wyoming, where his grandparents were from.

At J. C. Penney, bought me the clothes he wanted me to wear, in the image of himself, as a father does with his son.

Katharine, the half-sister I never knew, in Jackson, Wyoming, her long hug, not wanting to go because he'd probably told her she would not see him again—and I guess he wanted me to know her.

During the course of six days and six nights, and 2,859 miles (said my trip odometer), Gearhart taught me things he wanted me to know, trying, I guess, to make up for thirty-nine lost years.

Spending Father's Day together.

Eventually—and by now, emotionally spent, I've lost track of time—I return Pablo to the car and numbly walk a block and a half over to Center Street to American River Bank and wait my turn for a teller.

"Uh, I have this key," I say, holding it up. "It was given to me. I assume I'm supposed to access something here."

She glances at the key, studies my face. "I'll get the manager."

Ah, this is the part where I get arrested and thrown in jail for trying to steal a dead man's booty.

The manager, a little blond guy with glasses and a suit, appears in my face. "Do you have any ID?"

"Uh, yeah." I fumble with my wallet and show him my driver's license.

He looks at it, nods. "Follow me."

We go around the counter and into a windowless room.

"May I have your key?" he asks.

He uses mine and one of his own to unlock a slot, pulls out a metal drawer, and places it on a table nearby.

"Let me know when you're finished," he says, turning on his heel, closing the door behind him to give me some privacy.

I sit, staring at The Drawer.

Finally, I reach in, pluck out a square wooden box, which I unclasp. Inside, a ribbon in red, white, and blue and a medal, the Distinguished Intelligence Cross: *For a voluntary act or acts of extraordinary heroism including the acceptance of existing dangers with conspicuous fortitude and exemplary courage, awarded to Charles Gearhart, an employee of the Central Intelligence Agency.*

I stare at it in total awe and astonishment.

Next, a soft leather pouch filled with something heavy. I loosen its lace and tug it open. Inside, two fistfuls of gold coins, all the same, emblazoned with an Indian head on one side, a buffalo on the other.

Finally, a short stack of letters bound together with a rubber band. All of them addressed to *Luke Andersen* at different addresses where I've lived throughout my life—Bolinas, Solvang, Goleta, Summerland—with return addresses from foreign countries—France, Lebanon, Iraq—stamped but not postmarked, never sent.

And that's not all. When I'm checking out of Hotel Healdsburg, the front desk clerk hands me an envelope. I rip it open and find a handwritten letter on stationery from the Oxford Hotel in Bend dated *Father's Day.*

Dear Luke,

The greatest tragedy of my life was not being in yours, not watching you grow from birth into a man.

In some strange way, I think you have accomplished this over the past six days.

I tried to find the right moment to tell you face-to-face that you are my son, but my life has been one of keeping secrets. Revealing them has never been my strong suit.

Plus this: I didn't know how you felt about my absence in your life. And I wanted to spend time with you so much, I did not want to risk having you turn your back on me.

I love you, son. I always have.

Dad

I truly don't know what to do next. So I find myself thinking, what would Gearhart—*my dad*—do?

"There's no crisis," he told me in Wyoming, "that can't be solved with a martini and a cigar."

So I stroll over to the Healdsburg Bar & Grill and take a seat on the patio, order a Hendrick's martini, just the way Gearhart would—up, a twist, leave the shaker—and light the Macanudo he left me.

Afterward, I drive south, still numb, a jumble of emotions—all except one: as I penetrate a violent thunderstorm over Salinas, I find myself no longer scared, but oddly serene.

FATHER'S DAY:
ONE YEAR LATER

Forty one-ounce gold coins—one for each year of my life—equated to well over fifty grand.

I cashed in all but one.

First thing I did was buy Abe from the The Drive Cycle, and give him the best detailing and tune-up he ever had, and vowed that I would never, ever part with him. Instead, I'd take a road trip every new season, explore and discover and learn new things about life and nature.

Next, I made a down payment on a shop in Summerland—*Surf-dog*—to sell surfboards, including a line I design myself and produce in-house. The company mascot is Pablo, and our logo features him on a surfboard hanging ten.

One day out of five, I hire myself out to clients who need to repair their reputations on the Internet. I'm in higher demand than I want to be, so I'm training others, building a service.

Stephanie from Boise came out to see me about a month after Gearhart passed—and we moved in together a week later. She handles the books and runs the online surfboard shop.

My half-sister Katherine visited last Thanksgiving. We're coaxing her to take a break from buffalo and open an art gallery in Santa Barbara, and maybe she will.

Clean of weed for twelve months.

My mom confirmed it all, and added a few things Gearhart didn't say. Like, they'd met at the Monterey Jazz Festival, September 1974, while Dizzy Gillespie blew his trumpet onstage, and I got conceived soon after. She said she didn't tell him of my existence until I was five years old because she did not want to burden him or interfere with his career. And after that, without her even asking, he sent a check every month, without fail, to help cover the cost of raising me. It wasn't a lot, she said, but it helped.

I carry the remaining gold coin in my pocket every day to remember my dad.

One day it will belong to my son, Charlie Gearhart Andersen, born just a month ago.

Oh, I never heard back from the Montana Highway Patrol. I'd bet my good fortune that the guileful Gearhart fixed that one, too.